SECRETS BEYOND
SCYMARIA

Secrets Beyond

Scymaria

10 Oct 15
To Ana-
Enjoy the beginnings
of the series!
dj Smith

dj jameson smith

Library of Congress Control Number:		2013915294
ISBN:	Hardcover	978-1-4836-8889-3
	Softcover	978-1-4836-8888-6
	Ebook	978-1-4836-8887-9

This book was printed in the United States of America.

Rev. date: 08/29/2013

To order additional copies of this book, contact:
Xlibris LLC
1-888-795-4274
www.Xlibris.com
Orders@Xlibris.com
59704

CONTENTS

DEDICATION

This book is dedicated to the memory of my father, Walter T. Jameson Sr., for his support and continued reminders that I need only remember all things are possible when put into God's hands.

ACKNOWLEDGMENTS

FIRST AND FOREMOST, I want to thank my family and friends for putting up with my insane schedule and babbling for so long as I struggled through the creation of this book. Without their support, it simply would not have happened. My four beta readers, Thomas Frederick, Nan Madruga, Henriette Diouf, and Sarah Pruitt, were incredibly helpful. Their invaluable critiques, keeping it concise and real, made my editing journey much easier. My new artist friend, Michele Littlejohn-Luccketta, designed a beautiful watercolor scene for my cover and captured and created an excellent image for my photo on the book. Her creativity is a blessing! Last but not least, I want to thank the staff at Xlibris for their help pulling this first endeavor off—I could not have done it without each and every one mentioned.

This journey has just begun. There will be more to come.

Secrets Beyond Scymaria

Book One

CHAPTER ONE

The Dream

ONE LATE, WET spring morning not so long ago, two figures rushed down the sidewalk to the nearby park, buried in their coats for warmth. Deep in the Midwest, in a small college town forgotten by the rest of the world, the chill of the air drew icy clouds between them as they spoke, and it trailed behind as they hurried along. It was only a few blocks from their homes, and they were eager to get there. Each held their precious cargo tucked under the jacket, tight to their body. The two whispered almost the whole way. As Amy scrambled to keep up with Ty's long strides, her eyes grew bigger. Her usual optimistic smile was now gone.

Coming to a stop, she gasped, "No!" A dense veil hung in the still air, building a foggy wall between them, then dissipated.

"Yes!" Ty emphasized his statement with a jerk of his head. His black cap, usually hidden by and buried firmly amid his shoulder-length curly hair, flopped down into his face. The hat seldom left his head, except while he was in school, of course.

He laughed as he pushed the cap back up on top of his head with his free hand and became serious once again. Tall and lanky, he was rather quiet, soft spoken, and at times, overly sensitive. Although he and Amy spent a great deal of time growing up together as next-door neighbors, he spent a lot of his free time in the nearby parks observing animals and was very much at home wandering through the forests of trees. Amy would come with him on many of his ventures into the woods to explore. All this time together, especially since they were now in junior high, created plenty of teasing from their friends.

Amy stared at Ty then looked down the street toward the park. With a flip of her pig-tailed head, she looked back at Ty, scrunching her face up.

"It can't be, Ty! It just can't be—it's too unreal." Her love of reading, especially mysteries, spilled over into her life as an excellent student; and as she grew older, she found herself noticing more and more details around her—just like her favorite mystery characters would. Although she loved a good mystery and someday wanted to solve her very own, this was much more fiction that fact. She shook her head.

"But it *is* real, Amy. I *know* it is," he stated with certainty, a frown creeping onto his face. Ty stood tall, with one hand on his hip, the other tightly holding the jar, and his head held high.

He looked down toward the park, now coming into view.

It was one of many large stately old parks in their little college town. This one, filled with many tall, overgrown trees, created a miniature forest. The trees were excellent for climbing, and there were plenty of bushes to use for camouflage—this had been their favorite place when they were younger, for a good game of hide-and-seek. Concealed among the tall bushes, near the center of the park, was a good-sized spring-fed pond with a few huge trees overhanging it, as if to protect it. Along the edges were patches of fresh green reeds and cattails, now peeking up out of the water after their winter's rest. Beyond that, patches of grass here and there, excellent for lying back and gazing up through the dappled shade into the sky overhead.

Ty long ago mastered skipping a rock all the way across this pond, working the stones just right. In the spring, the pond seemed to overflow with frogs and tadpoles. The two loved to listen to their never-ending songs. Although they could hear the croaking from their homes, they loved to catch the tadpoles every year, hoping to get them to reside in their backyard also. This spring was no different. It was now a tradition, even though they knew they were "too old" for this sort of thing. They enjoyed their time at the pond. Amy and Ty were there just the day before and brought home two jars chock-full of tadpoles to put into a makeshift pond, made from a decrepit-looking kiddy pool, in Ty's backyard.

They hurried on into the park and headed straight for their favorite spot. Amy hesitated, but Ty grabbed her arm, and together they plunged through the bushes to the pond. As they stood at the edge, Ty pulled the jar of tadpoles from inside his jacket. Very carefully, he put it on the ground. For a moment, Amy and Ty silently watched the tadpoles as they swam frantically around the edge of the jar, then Amy asked, "Ty, how do you know?"

Ty quickly glanced at Amy. She was watching him now, very intently. He looked back at the tadpoles.

Shrugging his shoulders, he responded, "Well, 'cause I saw it in a dream." Before Amy could answer, he added, "And you know plenty of my dreams seem to come true."

Amy shivered. "But this one's *fairy-tale* stuff, Ty. How can you believe this dream is real?"

Still watching the tadpoles, Ty answered, "I don't know. It just felt real. And I want to make sure"—he hesitated for a moment—"that we always have all the frogs, the pond . . . and"—pointing to the ancient-looking tree closest to the pond—"that tree. For some reason, that tree is important too."

Ty reached for the jar and carefully unscrewed the lid.

"I just want to make sure nothing happens, okay?" He poured the water and tadpoles back into the pond. Immediately, the tadpoles fled away from the edge and out of sight. Still holding his now-empty jar, he turned to Amy. "Now, put yours back."

Amy held her jar close to her body in a childish fashion, not really wanting to give it up. She wasn't sure she could believe Ty this time. "This is too crazy. Just how could there be such a big swamp thing in this dinky pond?" Her hand shot up to cover her mouth. She realized she'd said that out loud, although she hadn't meant to. She looked at Ty. He just stood there, his head down, holding the empty jar in his hands. The pond was so quiet. There was only an occasional frog croaking and the glistening rings made by the tadpoles that once again returned to the pond's edge.

"Oh, this really is crazy! But if it makes you feel better, here!" Amy pushed the jar into Ty's chest. She was mad, and as he quickly reached up to take hold of the jar, the force of her push caused him to drop his jar as he grabbed hers. He lost his footing, and he fell backward into the pond, jar and all. Amy giggled. Ty looked so funny sitting in the pond.

His cap, now very soggy, was once again down over his eyes, dripping water onto his face. He sputtered and tried to keep the water out of his mouth.

"Dang!" he shouted. "That tastes awful!"

Amy's jar of tadpoles was now floating in the pond well out of his reach. She giggled again.

Ty announced, "There's *nothing* funny about this! The water tastes really awful, Amy, and"—wiping his mouth as he stood up, he pulled his cap back up onto his head—"and how do I explain this"—with a sweeping gesture, he pointed to his muddy, wet clothes—"this muddy mess to my mother?"

Amy put her hands to her mouth, muffling her giggles. "Sorry" was all she said as she continued to snicker.

Suddenly, just as Ty was pulling himself out of the pond, mud sucking at his shoes as he approached the edge, Amy grew quiet. Ty looked up at her and saw her hands still up to her mouth, but the laughing face and quiet giggles were gone. What he saw were wide, wide eyes and a pale face as she stared beyond him. Her hands dropped from her opened mouth, and one hand pointed behind him. Ty tried to spin around quickly to see where Amy was pointing. The mucky pond edge sucked hard at his shoes, and he fell back into the water.

As he fell, he saw it.

"What—!"

"Shh!" whispered Amy. She pulled at Ty to help him break free from the muck.

"My shoes!" Ty exclaimed in a whispered cry as Amy dragged him away from the pond's edge. Away from *it*.

"Amy!" Ty whispered. "Let go! My shoes came off! I need to get them. Mother'll kill me if I leave them behind."

Amy held fast. "No, Ty! Not right now," she whispered. She hadn't taken her eyes off of the thing the whole time. "What do you think it is?" Curious but cautious, she watched it.

Ty stopped struggling and turned to study what appeared to be a rock at the far edge in the shallows. From the corner of his eye, Ty noticed the jar of tadpoles bobbing nearer and nearer to it. He turned his full attention back to the thing in the pond. "It *looks* like a rock," he whispered. But they had never seen any in the water and certainly not such a big one. The rock was dark in color, but wet algae glistened from it as if it had recently pushed itself up from the depths of the pond.

Kind of muddy looking, he thought. "Well, it looks like a rock," he repeated, "but where the heck did it come from—rocks don't just pop up like that out of nowhere . . . and it looks like it's moving!" He was noticing tiny ripples moving away from it in every increasing rings, like when he threw pebbles in and disturbed the water.

"Ty, let's get out of here!" Still holding on to him, her grip increased. It almost hurt. Ty looked at her with sympathy, but his curiosity was getting the better of him.

"Maybe your dream was real, Ty. But we need to go! Now!" Her eyes pleaded, but she could see he wasn't going to budge.

"Oh, Ty!" She shook her head, knowing that she was not going to change his mind, but she continued to hold fast to his arm.

Ty wanted to find out what this thing was. *Maybe my dream was real,* he thought. *Of course it was. But maybe I didn't get the whole picture.*

He spoke in a quiet and calm voice, "Amy, it'll be okay. I'm not leaving, but if you want to, go ahead. I understand. I . . ." He looked back at the rock thing. He gasped, "Look! It's bigger! Wow!"

As he stepped toward it, Amy's grip tightened further, causing pain. "Amy, let go. You're hurting my arm!"

Ty yanked his arm loose as Amy apologized, "I'm sorry. It's just that—"

She didn't have time to finish. The thing was now definitely moving toward them, and it startled Amy. She let out a yelp. Both of her hands and Ty's shot up to her mouth to muffle the sound, so all that came out was a quiet squeak. The thing stopped.

Again, Amy whispered an apology when her mouth was free of hands. "Sorry, Ty. I do want to stay, but please be careful." She was just as curious as Ty but wanted to err on the side of caution.

Ty nodded as he crept forward to the edge of the pond and, as quiet as possible, retrieved his shoes. They were covered with mud and green algae. He scraped off as much muck as possible, and as he slipped them on, water and mud oozed out. He just rolled his eyes and shook his head, sighing.

Now, he was ready to investigate.

Standing at the water's edge, the jar caught his eye once again. *Is it important to get the tadpoles out of the jar?* he wondered. He wasn't sure, but in his dream, returning the tadpoles to the pond was important. Curiosity flooded his mind.

Ty jumped and stifled a shout as Amy touched his shoulder. He'd been so deep in thought; he hadn't heard her calling his name, so she put her hand on his shoulder, not realizing he would respond that way.

"Sorry. I didn't mean to scare you, but look at it now," she whispered with cautious enthusiasm. It had continued its slow movement toward them and now stopped at the center of the pond. Ty was so focused on the jar he hadn't noticed its progress. "Ty, when you shouted, it stopped again. Is it afraid of us?"

Yes, he thought.

He felt a surge of confidence. Standing up straight, eyes still on the thing, saying boldly, "You know, I think you might be right." His voice kept rising as he saw the thing quiver and slowly withdraw to the other side. It seemed to move a bit faster as he spoke louder and louder.

"Yes," he shouted. He felt downright great. He'd figured it out. Ty raced around the pond to the other side to test his theory.

"Ty!" Amy shouted. "What are you doing?" She was keeping her distance from the pond and did not hide her concern. Ty was getting dangerously close to the edge—and way too close to this swamp thing.

"You're too close, Ty! Watch out!" They could see an increased speed of retreat from the center of the pond. Rapidly, the rock approached the far side. Ty too was almost to that very spot, at the edge of the pond.

Grinning broadly, he called, "Don't worry!" He made sure his voice was nice and loud to see if he was right. "You see, I *do* think it's afraid of us!" He was positive he was correct.

Ty's smile vanished as he came to a halt, not very far from the thing. He could see it very clearly now—much too clearly and way too close. And the rock continued to come even closer.

Ty yelled and waved his arms, "Go away!"

It didn't. It came closer still.

It really does look like a rock. Or maybe a shell—like a turtle's shell, he thought. Mesmerized by this thing, Ty did not hear Amy calling out to him. He found this curious rock thing fascinating. He wanted to know more.

Amy stood, watching and yelling warnings as the two approached each other. She couldn't stand it. Ty was walking straight into trouble. She couldn't just stand there. She shouted one more time. He wasn't listening to her, and it had no effect on the creature. She ran as fast as she could around the pond toward Ty. She kept trying to get his attention as she approached the two.

Ty and the thing had reached the edge of the pond. Ty on land and the strange creature in the water. At the edge, with no more than a few feet between the two, they came to a stop. Amy could see Ty's hand reach out.

She screamed, "No, Ty, no!"

It seemed to reach out too. Something resembling a hand and then an arm began to grow out of this thing, reaching out toward Ty.

Just at the two touched, Amy tripped on a stump and went flying forward. As she fell, her head hit something hard. Her last sight, as she fell into darkness, was of Ty touching and being touched by the rock thing.

Ty's excitement grew. Here he was, standing in front of this creature!

Yes, he thought, *not a thing but a living creature. I can feel it!*

As he reached out, he was surprised but not afraid when he saw what looked like fingers and a hand slowly form and grow out from the rock. Then an arm . . . the forearm, elbow, and upper arm grew out, reaching out toward his own hand. Ty could feel a mixture of excitement and fear building in him. He could not stop himself. He *had* to touch it. A part of his mind was screaming for him to run away—to get away and be safe. But he needed to find out.

Instantly, he could feel a cool, tingling feeling in his hand as they touched. There was a feeling of calm coming over him. The fear gave way to this wonderful, restful feeling of peace. The tingling began to move up his arm.

It continued up his shoulder into his neck.

Too much, he thought. He broke the contact but didn't pull away too far. The thing didn't come forward . . . but neither did it retreat. The hand invited him to be touched once again.

Ty thought he heard something. He jerked his head toward the sound and was startled to see Amy sprawled on the ground, not moving.

His attention was fully on Amy now. He saw that her head had hit the edge of a rock. Forgetting the rock creature, he spun on his heels and raced to her side. She still didn't move.

"Amy!" Ty gently called to her as he checked the cut on her head. "Amy. Talk to me. Please, talk to me!"

He ran his hand across her injury.

Good. Only a little blood, he thought. *Well, it doesn't look too bad.*

He heard her moan, then he whispered her name again, "Amy. Talk to me. Are you okay?"

Amy's eyes fluttered and came open slowly. "Oh, my head . . ."

Ty put his hand on her shoulder and told her to lie still. He noticed her eyes kept opening wider and wider. Ty knew that look. He could feel something too. He turned slowly to where Amy was staring and, yes, standing over them was the rock thing. Towering over them. It had left the water, following Ty and now was only inches away. Amy stiffened slightly, not sure what to do. Ty quickly and quietly told Amy what happened, trying to reassure her.

His excitement was obvious. "Watch, Amy." He reached out to touch the rock. As he reached out, the rock again slowly grew fingers, then a hand and an arm. Again, the two touched. Ty had no fear this time.

Amy gasped, not because of what she saw but what she felt. Ty was still holding onto her shoulder when he touched the rock. A cool, tingling feeling, followed by a calmness she had not felt in a long time, came over her, and her throbbing headache seemed to vanish.

"Oh . . . my" was all she could manage.

CHAPTER TWO

Once Upon a Rock

AMY TOUCHED HER head where she hit the rock. She was still amazed that there was no cut, no pain, nor any lingering lump. It appeared to be healed.

"What do we do now, Ty?" They were both standing now, touching this rock thing. They talked, touched, examined, and talked. Any place they touched grew a 'hand' to extend out to meet their own hand. If they moved to a new spot, that one retreated into the rock, and a new hand came out wherever they reached.

"Rocky."

"What?" Ty looked over at her. He was puzzled.

"Rocky. We should call him Rocky." Amy had both of her hands holding two of Rocky's hands, slowly pumping them up and down, like a handshake. "How do you do, Rocky? My name is Amy, and . . ." She let go of one hand to point at her friend. "And this is Ty." Amy giggled with delight.

"Rocky? Really? You couldn't come up with something better than Rocky?"

Ty, laughing and shaking one of Rocky's hands, lowered his voice like an adult, saying, "How do you do, Rocky? It's very nice to meet you." Amy and Ty laughed together.

"Amy . . . Ty."

"What?" Ty exclaimed as he jumped back. The moment he and Amy jerked their hands away, Rocky's hands dissolved into its body.

"Did you hear that?" Ty stared at Rocky then turned to Amy. Amy returned his stare. Her mouth was wide open.

She stammered, "W-well, yeah, sort of, but I don't know." Her fingers touched her head and then came to rest on her chest, clutching at her shirt. "But I think I felt it too." A smile crept onto her face.

She paused, turned to look at the rock, and continued. "What did you hear? Could it . . . be . . . could it really be Rocky?"

Ty looked at Rocky, directing his question to their new "friend."

"Well, *can* you talk?" Silence. They looked at each other then back to Rocky.

Fingers began to form. "Amy, look! He's never done that before. I mean, we're not reaching out to him."

The hand formed, then the arm. It kept growing, reaching out. Ty and Amy stiffened. The arm grew longer than before, wavering back and forth as it tried to reach one of them. Ty finally reached his hand out.

Amy gripped his shoulder and whispered a quick "Careful."

As his hand touched Rocky's, a flood of words came to the two of them. As Amy jumped back, the words quieted in her mind. Quickly, she touched Ty's shoulder again. A jumble of words and images again poured into her head.

"It's in my mind, Ty. In my mind, not my ears," she whispered.

Nodding in agreement, he put his fingers to his lips. "Shh."

Ty was trying to make sense of what the rock was trying to say. At first, it was just a tangle of words; but slowly, after what felt like hours, both could make out some complete thoughts; and finally, Rocky made sense to both of them.

"Hello, Amy and Ty. How are you?"

"Hi." Ty was calm, but his mind raced. He couldn't believe he was carrying on a conversation with a talking rock. "What was that all about?" asked Ty, referring to the jumbled words. "I mean, I'm fine, but why didn't you talk to us before?"

"I was trying to teach you—before we could communicate, *you* needed to learn the fundamentals." The talking rock paused, then apologized, "I am sorry to cause so much fear."

Amy could feel that was directed at her. "Rocky, it's okay. I'm okay now. Thank you for helping me." Amy knew it was Rocky who had completely healed her injury and aching head.

"You are welcome. You were injured and needed help. But please. You may call me the Gua—"

Just then, in the distance, Amy heard a familiar voice interrupt him as they turned away from Rocky to see who was coming.

"Amy! Where are you?"

"Oh m' gosh! It's my mom!" Her eyes darted from Rocky to Ty. "What do we do now? If Mom sees Rocky, she's sure to freak out. Rocky! Quick! Back into the water!"

The rock had already begun his retreat.

"I'll go to her. That'll give Rocky time to hide." With that, Amy dashed off into the direction of her mom's voice, calling out to her, "Coming, Mom!"

Ty was standing at the pond's edge, dripping wet, with the jar of tadpoles in one hand and the lid in the other when Amy returned with her mom. Amy looked a bit anxious as they came into the clearing but broke out laughing when she saw how wet Ty was. Although the mud no longer caked his clothes, he was wet from head to toe.

Her mom stifled a laugh as he explained why they had come to the pond, apologizing with a quiet "Sorry."

He carefully left out their discovery and the details surrounding Rocky. She simply smiled at the absurdity of it all—the dream, Ty's need to release the tadpoles, and his crazy, sopping wet hat that covered half of his face. Amy kept flashing glances at the pond and at Ty who was remaining calm throughout it all.

Amy's mom patted him on the head, propped the hat back up on top, and laughed. "All I want to know is if you two want to have lunch at our house. I didn't think I would have to come on a safari to find you. Well, what do you think? Lunch is in one hour. Will you be there?"

Amy quickly whispered something in Ty's ear, and he nodded. She turned to her. "Mom, can we have a picnic lunch? I'll help put it together."

"Yes, you *may*," she corrected her daughter gently. "Let's get it ready."

Ty was left standing by the pond, still dripping wet as the two vanished among the bushes.

"That was close," he whispered as he sat down on a tuft of grass near the edge. He leaned over the pond with the jar, pouring the last of the tadpoles back into the water, wondering what it was their new friend had started to say—and if they'd ever see him again.

He sat on his tuft of grass, gazing at the glassy reflection of the overhanging tree, pondering. He had plenty of time to think. Amy wouldn't be back for a while.

What was this creature? Where did it come from? They had been there so many times before, so why did it choose today to show itself? He kept rolling these questions and many more over and over in his mind.

So lost in thought, Ty didn't notice Amy settle in beside him. "Hi! Penny for your thoughts."

Ty jumped up and nearly fell back into the muddy water.

"*Don't* do that!" He regained his balance and stared at Amy.

She laughed as she stood back up and looked around, searching for Rocky. Her arms were heavy with the basket brimming with picnic goodies. "Where is he? Did he come back?"

Ty answered with a shake of his head, took the basket from Amy, and set it down on a larger patch of grass, a short distance from the pond. In silence, the two set up their picnic spot. They just sat there, gazing into the pond. Slowly, without a word, they ate their lunch. Both were thinking about what happened.

"Ty?" Amy broke the silence with a hoarse whisper. "Did it really happen? I mean, did we really see, hear, and feel all that stuff? I'm not imagining things, am I?" She moved her gaze from the pond to Ty. Deep in thought, his staring eyes fixed on the pond.

"Ty?" Smiling, she reached out as a joke, waving her hand in front of his face. "Hello? Anybody home?"

Laughing, she put her hand gently on his shoulder. "Ty!" He still didn't respond.

It was no longer a joke. She was concerned.

She wondered, *Why is he zoning out like this?*

"What's the matter?" She shook him gently and waited a moment. "Ty, stop that! Talk to me, Ty!"

Slowly, Ty seemed to come back to reality. "Hmm? Oh . . . I . . . I'm sorry, Amy. I . . . I just . . ." He stopped and frowned. "I can't exactly say where I . . . I mean, what I was doing."

Amy scowled. She was really puzzled now.

Where? she thought. *No, he didn't mean to say 'where'—he meant 'what' he was doing . . .*

Ty interrupted her thoughts. He was explaining something. She focused on him.

" . . . And the next thing I knew, I was seeing all sorts of weird things and feeling so relaxed—just like when we were *touching* Rocky. I was really trying to concentrate on all of it—to make sense of what I was seeing . . . It was so unreal!"

His excitement was growing, and when Ty was excited about something, Amy found it quite irresistible and could easily get caught up in it.

She asked cautiously, "Do you think it was Rocky trying to talk to you?"

"Naw." He shook his head. "Remember, we could only hear him when we were touching him."

"Oh, yeah," she half mumbled. Amy wondered if that was the only way. "But what if that changed? What if now that we can talk to him by touching, he can also talk—"

Amy interrupted herself, excited.

"Ty—yesss! Remember, you said he could feel and hear us? Well, I'll bet now that he's taught us to understand him while we touch him, well, now he can talk to us without touching—like . . . like mental telepathy?"

All caution was gone now. Amy was sure, and now, it was Ty's turn to get caught up in her excitement.

"Yeah! Oh, Amy! It makes more sense that way. Drats! Now, what was he trying to tell me?" Ty took a few steps closer to the pond. How he wished the big rock would show itself. He stood at the water's edge, scanning the surface for any sign of him.

Amy came up from behind, pouting. "But why was it only *you* that heard him and not me?"

Ty turned around to see her frowning face. "Aw, Amy! You know how you can't listen in on whispers! Well, that's kinda like what this is, I guess. He's just whispering into my ear."

"I can try . . ." She continued to frown, trying unsuccessfully to hide her jealousy. "Well, why not whisper in *mine*?"

Shrugging his shoulders, Ty answered, "I don't know. Well, maybe because I was the first one he talked . . . to . . ." Ty turned back to the water as Amy started to say something. Ty raised his hand, signaling her to be quiet. She then realized that Rocky must be talking with Ty—again.

She pouted but waited quietly. She shut her eyes tight, trying to pick up on any little thought that might be out there. Nothing. She stood there a little bit longer, but her impatience won over. She found a stump near Ty and perched herself on it, watching him. He had moved even closer to the pond, the water lapping at his shoes. Slowly, he crouched down and mindlessly touched the surface of the water with his hand. All the time, he had a serene but blank gaze that appeared to be looking far away at something. His hand began to reach into the water. He reached deeper. The water came up to his elbow.

Cocking her head, she wondered how he'd found such a deep spot so close to the edge.

A snap of branches behind them startled Amy. She spun around, nearly falling off the stump in the process, to see two of their friends coming into the clearing.

"Hey, Amy! Ty! Whatcha up to?"

Quickly jumping off the log, Amy slipped over to Ty, nudging him with her foot and hoping it wouldn't be as hard as last time to get his attention. He responded quickly by rising up, turning around and waving, water dripping from his arm.

She sighed in relief and said, "Oh, not much. We've just had a picnic lunch my mom made and goofin' around with the tadpoles. Not too many today, though." As if on cue, the tadpoles seemed to disappear into the depths. Only a very few remained—near Ty.

"Gee, you're right!" one of the friends exclaimed as he hunted the pond edge. He managed to catch one and released it.

"Well, that's no fun! Hey, Ty . . . Amy, wanna come and play some ball on the Green? We've gathered together a team, and we're two short. Wanna play?"

As the other friend tossed a ball up into the air, a strange gust of wind caught it. It landed near the edge of the pond where Ty stood. He leaned over, scooped it up, and tossed it back to his friend, saying, "Naw. Looks like it might be too windy on the Green to play anyway."

He looked toward Amy. "Besides, I have to help Amy get all this stuff together and back to her house, or her mom'll have a fit."

Amy could tell he was trying to gracefully weasel his way out of the game. His eyes still had a bit of that far-off look she'd seen before. She hoped their friends didn't notice and wondered if he was still hearing things.

She piped up with a smile, "Yeah, Ty promised to help get this stuff back, and I'm *not* going to let him off the hook!" She laughed lightheartedly and turned to pick up a few items.

"Fine. Suite yourself. Come on, Mike." The two turned away from the pond and called out, "See you later!"

Amy and Ty waved, then busied themselves in earnest with the task of cleaning up their picnic spread until their friends were well out of sight.

"Oh, man! That was close! Ty, are you okay? What happened? Can you still hear something? I mean—"

Ty interrupted Amy's chatter and stopped working. "Yes, I can still hear something—quiet—please."

After a few moments, he shook his head.

"It's gone, now." He plopped down on the half-folded blanket, put his head in his hands with his elbows resting on his knees. He slowly shook his head and quietly said, "So many weird thoughts . . . They're so hard to put together. I just can't figure them out yet. What's he trying to tell me?"

"Well, *maybe*," she said with a grin, "we need to write them down and look at them like a detective would." She was sure this was the right thing to do. Her eyes gleamed with excitement. The thought of treating this like one of her mysteries intrigued her.

"Oh, you and your mystery books!" Looking up at Amy, Ty had a smile on his face. He knew how much she loved a good mystery.

And, boy, he thought, *this sure is a mystery!*

"Well, okay," he finally said. "Got anything to write on?" Ty really knew better than to ask that. He laughed as Amy pulled out a small notebook and pencil from her back pocket. She was aglow.

This is what she'd always wanted to do. Solving a mystery, like Miss Marple, or her favorite detective, Sherlock Holmes, thrilled her. This was her chance to hunt down clues to crack this mystery.

"Okay, Ty." Flipping her pigtails back out of the way and with pencil and notebook ready, she looked and sounded so professional that Ty gave a chuckle but settled into her questioning. He tried to answer her questions in as much detail as possible. As Amy fired off question after question, Ty finished picking up their spread, placing it all in the overflowing picnic basket as he answered her barrage of questions.

He now carried the loaded basket while Amy, holding only pencil and pad, kept asking questions and writing answers as they headed for her house.

They were halfway up her front steps when Amy turned and cried out, "Oh no!"

Her abrupt stop caused Ty to bump into her, and he nearly dropped the picnic supplies.

As he made an effort to rebalance his load, he grumbled, "Amy, *please* don't do that. I almost dropped all this stuff!"

Amy apologized as she helped Ty deposit everything on the front porch table. She lowered her voice and asked, "Ty, what if he comes back, and we're not there?"

He pondered that for a moment before responding. "No, I feel like that's not a problem. I don't know why. I don't know for sure if or when he'll come back, but I hope he will—I think he'll let us know."

Amy's shoulders slumped noticeably. She hadn't thought about that. "Not come back? Oh, no! That's even worse. Now we've really gotta figure this out—I mean, figure out a way to talk to him and get him to talk to us in a way we understand!"

Scribbling faster, she opened and dove through the door, not even waiting for Ty to follow. The screen door slammed in his face.

"Hey! Wait, Amy!" As he fumbled with the door, he could see Amy running up the stairs, two at a time, heading for her room at the top of the stairs. The screen door slammed shut behind him as he started to follow her, but the moment his feet hit the steps, he heard Amy's mom calling.

"Amy? Is that you?" As the kitchen door opened, Ty knew he'd better stay and talk to her. "Hi, Mrs. Taylor."

"Oh, Ty! I take it Amy's already upstairs?" She didn't wait for an answer. She shook her head and chuckled as she continued to talk. "Did you and Amy have a nice picnic lunch?"

"Yes, ma'am, it was great. Thank you. We just got back." He pointed to the front porch and asked, "I left the stuff on the porch. Should I bring it in?"

"Yes, please, Ty. Bring it into the kitchen and help yourself to some of the cookies on the counter. They just came out of the oven—your favorite!"

Ty gave a sniff as he opened the screen door. Wafts of deliciousness escaping the kitchen finally reached him. "Mmm! Chocolate-chunk cookies! Thanks! I'll get some for Amy too, if that's okay." He was halfway into the kitchen with the picnic supplies by then.

"Certainly!" Mrs. Taylor was back to work in the kitchen making other scrumptious-smelling goodies. "Here," as she cleared a space on the kitchen table, "please put the basket over here."

After depositing the basket, Ty grabbed two handfuls of cookies. "Thanks again, Mrs. Taylor. Amy and I will be in her room for a while." As he hurried out of the kitchen, he shoved a cookie into his mouth, climbed the stairs three at a time, and was in Amy's room in no time at all.

"What took you so long?" Amy was sitting cross-legged on her bed, grinning, with her hand outstretched, waiting for Ty to unload the goodies into it.

"What makes you think any of this is for you? I had to bring all the picnic stuff into the kitchen all by myself."

Amy's outstretched hand remained, fingers wiggling slightly along with the smile.

He rolled his eyes and pretended to eat one of her cookies. She leapt from her bed, hand still out, and made a little squeal in protest. Ty laughed and handed her the cookies. As she popped one into her mouth, a muffled "thank you" could be heard . . . along with a chuckle. Amy settled back onto the bed, and Ty grabbed a chair, dragging it over near the bed. The two settled into the business of studying the notes Amy took earlier that day. In the background, they could hear Amy's mom clanking pots and pans in the kitchen, and the aroma of more freshly baked cookies permeated the open bedroom door.

CHAPTER THREE

New Discovery

EACH DAY, VERY early in the morning before school, the two dashed off to the park, hoping to summon the rock back. Each day, they left saddened because they neither saw nor heard from him. They even tried after school with the same negative results. Two weeks dragged by without any response from their mysterious friend. Their classmates started to tease them even more than usual.

Their parents voiced concerns over schoolwork possibly suffering from their lack of attention. Amy and Ty assured them they were fine and tried hard to concentrate on the lessons at school. They hurried through their homework each night so there would be time to discuss their plan of action for the next day. Finally, another Friday came. There was a sense of relief for both of them. They knew they would have more time now—two whole days.

As the end of the school day approached, their science teacher, Miss Tansy, asked for everyone's attention. "Now then, class, I know it's Friday, and we are nearing the end of the school year." She paused to focus on two boys snickering in the back. They stopped immediately.

"As I was saying . . ." She eyed the two and continued, "There is one more important report that needs to be completed before the end of school. We talked about this last week." There were moans from all corners of the class.

"This report will weigh heavily on your final grade, so I do hope you've been thinking about what your subject will be. Remember that it can be done on anything in the natural science field, and you are to buddy up into teams of two. How many of you still need to choose a partner?"

Several hands shot up, and as Miss Tansy assisted in matching up the few remaining teams, Ty shot a glance at Amy. They had long since decided to team up but hadn't chosen a subject yet. Amy was all smiles. Ty knew she'd decided on a topic with that grin. And he had a feeling he knew exactly what the subject was too.

He shook his head and mouthed the word, "No."

She scowled.

"Too much fiction, not enough science," he whispered.

She started to answer but stopped. Her mouth clamped shut. Her eyes darted up toward the teacher. Ty quickly turned his attention to Miss Tansy who had finished her matchmaking and was now watching Ty. She quietly removed his hat and returned to the front of the classroom, placing it on her desk.

"You may pick it up after class, Ty."

His face reddened.

"Now, what's too much fiction and not enough science? Perhaps I can help sort it out for you . . ." Her eyes slowly settled onto Amy. "Both of you."

Now, the whole class was watching Ty and Amy. Under their teacher's scrutiny, both turned beet red, and each could feel the heat.

"W-well," stuttered Ty. "It's nothing, really. We'll figure out if it's something we can use in our report—later."

Miss Tansy was still watching Amy, now completely recovered, wearing an enormous grin on her face. "Miss Tansy, if we were to find a new species, could we use that for our report?"

Ty fixed a cold stare on Amy. She ignored him and continued, "I mean . . . Well, could we?"

There were whispers all over the room.

Miss Tansy was taken aback only momentarily and replied, "Why, yes, Amy."

She paused for a moment, certain that whatever Ty and Amy discovered could not possibly be new and added, "Even if you find out it's not a new species, you may still do your report on it. You might want to include the steps you needed to go through to verify what species it is."

Taking advantage of this strange question, she continued, "But if it is new, you need to follow the proper procedures. To do that, you could contact the college zoology department. The department head—I believe his name is Professor Larkin—has just completed an important paper on new species. I'm sure he'd be more than happy to assist you."

Amy, even more confident, said, "Thanks, Miss Tansy," and turned to taking notes on what her teacher said. Ty, slumping in his seat momentarily, realized it might draw Miss Tansy's attention again and straightened himself.

"You're welcome, Amy." Turning her attention to the class, she said, "Now that that is settled, the due date for this report is May first. That will give you plenty of time to finish your reports and time for me to grade them before school lets out for the summer."

As Miss Tansy wrote the due date on the blackboard, the bell rang. With a nod from their teacher, the class piled out the door to freedom. A whole two days of freedom! There was scurrying and yelling in the halls as students dashed to catch their busses or to find friends and begin their walk homeward.

Amy and Ty took their time gathering their books together. They wanted time alone—time for their friends to go ahead without them as they'd done these last two weeks. But today, in doing that, they hadn't reckoned on the curiosity roused in Miss Tansy. As they quietly headed through the door, she called out to them. "Ty. Amy."

"Now we're in for it," he groaned in a whisper.

"Not necessarily. Let me handle it," whispered Amy. They both turned quickly to her call.

"Yes, Miss Tansy?" Smiling, Amy knew exactly what to say.

Fully aware that they might not want the whole class to know what their project was, Miss Tansy waited until now to probe further. She also held Ty's hat in her extended hand.

"Ty, here's your hat." Ty thanked her as he took possession of it.

"I'm just curious. Now that the class is gone, will you share with me this discovery of yours?"

Amy glanced at Ty who was looking rather helpless. Turning to her teacher, she slowly responded, "Well, honestly, I think we'd rather not say until we've researched things further. We're going over to the college and talk to that professor as soon as we get our homework done, so we really need to be going." Amy waved good-bye with one hand and pushed Ty out the door with the other.

"G'bye, Miss Tansy!" both called out as they rounded the corner. They didn't want their teacher to dig any deeper. Then they ran most of the way to their homes.

Slowing to a walk and out of breath, only about two houses from Ty's home, he shook his head and muttered, "Oh, man! I don't want to repeat that anytime soon! I was afraid she was going to make us tell her about Rocky."

Even Amy, as confident as she had been, wasn't sure how much Miss Tansy was going to ask. She was glad their teacher didn't pry too much.

"Yeah. But, Ty, it may not be over. Come Monday, she may ask more questions." Pausing to think about it for a moment, she added, "Well, maybe not Monday, but after we've talked to the professor, she might get curious. We'll put that off as long as possible—and come up with something."

As the two turned up the walk to Ty's home, he added, "Maybe she might even forget!"

Amy only had to think about it for a half second, shaking her head laughing. "Nope, don't think that's likely. You and I, unfortunately, are pretty good students, and she always seems to be interested in what we've got going on. She's a pretty smart teacher. We're going to have to be careful about what we say."

They climbed the stairs onto the porch. "Want to do homework on the porch or in the kitchen?" Ty was hoping she'd say the kitchen. Their friends wouldn't be able to see them.

"The porch," she responded as she plopped her books down on the table. "You get the goodies." She pulled out the homework assignment and busied herself as Ty stood there scowling. He wished he hadn't offered a choice. Amy glanced up. "Don't worry so much, Ty. Just go get the goodies."

"How do you do that?" It always amazed him when she knew what he was thinking.

"Do what?" Amy stopped organizing her work.

"How do you know what I'm thinking?"

Amy laughed. "I don't. I just know you're a worrier, and if you're not going to get the goodies from your mom, you must be worried. So stop worrying and get going already."

Ty shrugged and went inside, mumbling something.

Amy could see some of her friends walking by. They waved, and she waved back. Amy's best friend, Amanda, was with the group. Amanda broke away as they passed by.

"See ya," she called to them as she hurried up the walk to Ty's house.

Just then, Ty came out with a tray full of fruit, cookies, and two glasses of lemonade. "Oh, great," he whispered with clenched teeth, wanting to turn around and go back inside.

Amy quietly said, "Shh!" Smiling, she greeted Amanda, "Hi, buddy! Whatcha up to? Want to join us?"

She heard a little moan from Ty as he put the tray down.

"Sure . . . if it's okay with Ty." Amanda knew Ty was painfully shy around most girls, and she didn't want to intrude.

"It's okay. Ty, please get another glass for 'Manda, okay?" She smiled at Ty. It was a smile that asked him to go along with it.

Ty mumbled, "Sure." He turned on his heels and went in to get the lemonade, wondering what Amy had up her sleeve now.

With Ty inside, Amanda rushed up the stairs and slipped into the seat beside Amy. Quietly, she asked, "Mee, what's with you and Ty? Miss Tansy looked like she was going to eat you alive!"

Amanda popped a piece of apple in her mouth. "Mmm . . . Sweet!"

Amy signed. "Oh, Miss Tansy was fine. It's just that we're not sure what it is we've found and didn't want to look dumb. Her idea of going to the college was great. After our homework, we're going to go over there."

Amanda nibbled on her second piece of fruit and added, "Well, I'm sure you'll figure it out. I've got to get home and do *my* homework too! Good luck! See you later—call me when you get home, and we can talk for a while!"

She grabbed a couple of cookies as Ty came onto the porch with the extra glass of the lemonade. "Bye, Ty. Can't stay, but thanks for the food!"

She flew down the stairs, down the walk, and out onto the sidewalk, waving the cookies as she went.

"Boy, she sure doesn't stay in one place long!" He looked at the glass in his hand, shrugged his shoulders, and put it on the table. As he sat down, grabbing a cookie, he asked, "So what's up?"

Amy had just popped some fruit in her mouth and giggled. She held her hands up, smiling, and finally was able to say, "Problem solved!"

"And what does that mean?" Ty wasn't sure what Amy said to Amanda. He wasn't sure he wanted to know.

"Well, I love her to bits, but you know how 'Manda likes to know what's going on and how she likes to share that information—"

Ty interrupted sarcastically, "Yep. She loves bein' nosey and telling everybody everything." He rolled his eyes and made faces.

"Ty. That's not nice! Anyway, I just told her we didn't want to look dumb. She'll pass that around, and all will be fine." Amy felt quite satisfied with the outcome.

The look on Ty's face was one of skepticism.

"Oh, Ty. Just relax. Here. Read this." She passed him the notes she'd written down about the college. "As soon as we're done with our homework, we'll go. Okay?"

Ty read over the information Amy had taken those last few minutes in class. Reluctantly, he said, "Well, okay."

The two hurried through what little homework they had, and after informing his mother, they headed for the college. On the way, they stopped at the pond. Still, no luck trying to talk to Rocky.

CHAPTER FOUR

The Professor

"WELL, THAT'S JUST great!" grumbled Ty. "He thinks we're pulling his leg. He doesn't believe us! Now what?"

Amy was unhappy with the interview too. They were careful to leave out the details that would identify their friend in any way. Dr. Larkin really seemed to be a nice guy, but it was obvious he didn't take them seriously when he stopped them mid-discussion and escorted them to the door. "At least we got the information about how to identify new species like Miss Tansy wanted. Maybe we were too vague," she sighed. "I thought I asked good questions. I even showed him some of my—oh no, Ty!"

Amy stopped in her tracks. "My notebook! I laid it down on his desk while we were talking. We've got to go back and get it!"

"Amy. It's probably too late! Amy!" It was a wasted effort. She was already turning around and running full speed toward the college. With his longer legs, Ty quickly caught up with her, and the two ran with all their might, back to his building.

As they ran down the hall to Dr. Larkin's office, a janitor stepped out in front of them, holding out a wet mop, causing the two to nearly collide with him.

Dropping his mop, he grabbed each of them by their arm, demanding, "Hold on there, kids! This is a college, not a playground. Just where do you think you're going?"

Ty gasped, "To . . . to Dr . . . . Larkin's office. We . . ."

"Just what business do you two have with him?"

"Oh, please . . . sir." Amy was still out of breath but tried to explain. "We . . . we waited an hour to see him . . . Then we . . . we left our notes in . . . in his office. You can ask him yourself. Please," she pleaded, "we need those notes for a class assignment." She sighed deeply as she caught her breath.

The janitor told them to wait. He disappeared into the professor's office. A few minutes later, he emerged, motioning for them to enter.

They quietly walked into the office. Ty turned to see the door close behind them. Dr. Larkin sat at his desk with the notebook in his hand. "Is this what you're looking for?" He waved the notebook momentarily and then opened it up. "There's more in here than you told me, Amy. It's very interesting. Just where did you see this thing?"

Amy and Ty looked at each other with determination. They had promised each other not to say where it was. They both nodded and turned to look at the professor.

Amy spoke first. "Sir, to protect him—or it, we have decided it's not safe to say where we found him—I mean, it."

She felt very nervous all of a sudden. This nice man had changed. He ran his fingers through his wild red hair. Though all smiles, this well-dressed man in a dark purple, pin-striped suit that hung on his body like a lanky scarecrow, seemed to be, well, very devious, she decided. When they first met, he was so attentive, listening to them, politely answering their questions. Now, Amy was glad their park was not the only one in town with a pond. In fact, the town was peppered with ponds, and she was glad she hadn't mentioned which one in the notes.

"Amy and Ty." He was speaking very slow, still smiling, trying to control his words and anger. His hand went back up to his hair, smoothing it once again.

"How am I to believe you if you don't plan on telling me where I can find this creature?"

"But, sir, you already told us you don't believe us. Could we please have our notes back?" Ty stretched his hand out to receive the notebook.

Dr. Larkin held onto it, holding it in one hand and tapping his other opened hand with it. "Amy, you keep excellent notes" is all he said.

"Thanks," she mumbled.

Aside from the tapping, there was no sound. A door slammed down the hall, making both Amy and Ty jump.

"Sir, please?" Ty still had his hand out, eager to receive it. His eyes stared steadily into Dr. Larkin's. Ty was not going to let the professor scare him.

Amy couldn't stand it. All the quiet was too much. She had thought it all out.

"Sir," she began. The professor continued to lock his gaze on Ty. She cleared her throat, and he turned to face her.

"Dr. Larkin, we don't even know if we can find him—I mean, it—again. It's there in the notes. It refuses to contact us, so there's no way to find it. So the notes really won't do any good until we *can* find it." Cringing, she knew she had said too much. As an afterthought, she added, "And we really need the notebook for our assignment."

Dr. Larkin stopped tapping and looked down at the notebook. He was thinking.

Ty looked at Amy. She nearly gasped but held it back. Ty had that distant look. Again. But this time, panic mingled with it as he saw Amy's expression. He tried to bring himself back but failed.

"Excuse me, sir. I-I'm not feeling very good," he stuttered as he hid his face by turning away.

Before Dr. Larkin could get a good look at him, Ty slipped out of the room, leaving the door ajar. Amy's head began to whirl with what was happening. What she needed was a plan.

She made herself concentrate. "Oh, please, sir. Ty is sick, and I need to go with him, but I really need that notebook for school."

The professor grew concerned. "Well, perhaps." He started to hand it to her and hesitated.

"No, let's go find him. We can't have him wandering the halls." He rose from his chair, placing the notebook on the desk.

Amy's mind was screaming. What could she do? Now was her chance. Like greased lightning, she grabbed the notebook, dashed through the open door, and slammed it behind her. She could hear the professor shouting for her to stop. Her heart pounded so hard it felt like her chest might explode any second. She ran as fast as she could, hoping that Ty was doing the same.

Her feet slamming against the tile floor echoed as she ran down the long hall and out the front door like a slingshot. She darted toward a road that paralleled the one she would usually take. She didn't want Dr. Larkin to know where she was going. She quickly cut to the left where she'd normally go right.

"Just in case," she thought aloud. Her lungs and legs were screaming at her. They hurt, but she kept going.

Now, back to the right, she thought. She slowed as she approached the intersection. She stopped. Gasping for air, she watched two cars approach. One was the college security car. Hoping they didn't see her, she ducked into some bushes. They pricked her head and tangled in her pigtails as she crouched among them. The two cars passed. She stayed in hiding, while she caught her breath.

At least the cars were going in the wrong direction, she thought.

When they were safely out of sight, and she could breathe a bit easier, she checked cautiously to make sure it was safe. The intersection was clear. After freeing her hair from the tangled bushes, she dashed across the street and down a block. Then she cut through an alley until she came to the right intersection. Again, cautiously, she looked around. Not a car in sight. She sighed. She could see the park only a few blocks away on the other side of the street. She decided to cut through more yards instead of walking on the sidewalk. Once she reached the park, she slipped into the heavily wooded section.

Now protected by the cover of the park, she finally felt safe. She worked her way through, reaching the thicket of bushes that hid the pond, and paused. She looked around. Listening and seeing nothing suspicious, she slipped through the bushes. Standing at the edge, she peered into the clearing. The pond reflected the late afternoon sun's shadows through the dappled light. She couldn't see anyone.

"Ty!" she called out in a hoarse whisper.

"Ty!" No response. Then she recalled the difficulty she had getting his attention when he had *that* look.

Oh, no, she thought. *He'll never hear me!*

"Ty, where *are* you?"

She stepped out and carefully moved toward the pond, looking everywhere. The pond was unusually still, which made her very nervous. She looked into the pond and up into the massive branches of the huge, old trees scattered around the pond. She looked behind each tree. Amy grew increasingly alarmed.

Again, her mind screamed at her. She took a deep breath to help calm down. A horrible thought crept into her mind. She kept pushing it away, but it continued to linger, and she began to panic.

What if, she thought, *oh, what if Ty never left the building? What if he went searching for a bathroom or something!*

Another very long, deep breath. And another. She sat down on the log near the pond where she had watched Ty try to talk to Rocky. Her mind was muddled with thoughts. Tears welled up, blurring her vision. She wiped her eyes.

"Ty . . . Ty, where are you? Rocky, please help me!" Now she focused her thoughts on their experience two weeks ago. She thought only of Ty and Rocky.

Amy. She jumped to her feet and spun around—all the way around, but nobody was there.

Amy.

She froze in her tracks and whispered, "Ty, is that you? Where are you?"

She turned around, carefully scanning all about her until her eyes came to rest on the old, monstrous tree. It was one she, along with every other kid in town, was told to avoid because of the danger of it falling down. It was *very* old. And very big too. She felt the need to come closer. Her fingers touched her head.

She could hear something, she thought. Or was it that she felt it? She wasn't sure, but she was drawn closer and closer to this massive, old tree. Was it the tree that was 'talking' to her?

Oh, this is crazy, she thought with a half smile.

Amy. There it was again. She wondered if it was coming from the tree.

"Ty, is that you?" she said it in such a small whisper no one could have heard it.

Yes! Amy. I finally did it! Keep coming this way . . . And don't be afraid.

Did what? Afraid, she thought, *of what?*

"What?"

That's just it. There's nothing to be afraid of! Touch the tree, Amy. Touch it, Ty urged.

Amy hesitated. Looking around to make sure it was safe, she slowly reached out, not sure of what to expect. She wondered if the tree responded like Rocky, sprouting hands. She stopped.

No, Amy. Keep coming. Don't worry, Ty reassured her.

"Ty! Where are you? That Dr. Larkin is after us."

I know, said Ty. *Just keep coming closer. Hurry up.*

Amy thought about this. They'd never gotten any closer than arms length to Rocky. She wondered what would happen.

Just wait and see! Ty exclaimed. She could feel his laughing eyes and smiling face.

"Okay. Here goes." She closed her eyes, placed one hand straight out in front of her, and moved the other hand up near her face so she wouldn't scrape her nose. She moved up to the point where she felt she must be nose-to-nose with the tree. She braced herself for an abrupt stop that never came. She scowled, dropped her hand, and opened her eyes.

"Wha . . . ?" She expected to see tree bark right under her nose. Instead, what she saw before her was a colorful meadow that seemed to be alive with movement, a peaceful-looking forest full of towering trees, ferns, and other underbrush, all bathed in a shimmering, soothing light. The entire wall standing before her framed this beautiful scene. She spun back around, and what she saw, through more shimmering light, was their pond, the trees, and the bushes.

"Oooh! My! Gosh! This is beyond amazing!"

"You were always one to understate things!" Amy spun around again to see Ty standing there with a huge grin plastered across on his face.

"Ty! Where'd you come from? That is you, isn't it? Please tell me it is you! I . . ." Amy lunged at him, giving him a hug. She was so glad to see him.

"Yeah, it's me. Are you okay? I'm sorry I left you like that. I didn't think it would have been too good an idea for me to stick around with Rocky's voice in my head—not with what you've told me about how I act."

"You're right, Ty. You kinda glazed over when he looked down. I'm glad you left." Amy pulled the notebook out and waved it in the air. "But—I did get this back."

"Good. They're safe then . . ."

"They?" Amy was confused. "What do you mean 'they'?"

"Rocky's not the only one here. This tree is part of a group, I think. I'm not sure how many there are, and they haven't been very helpful when I ask questions."

"Why?" Amy's calmness was overridden by a touch of curiosity, with a little edge of fear mixed in.

Ty shrugged. "Rocky said to wait till you were here so he could tell us both—together."

"So . . ." Amy turned slowly, looking around. "We're here—together, Rocky. What's going on?"

Amy felt a rush of warmth overcome her. She felt quite light-headed, and her knees felt wobbly. Then crumpling to her hands and knees, she said, "Whoa! Now, that was weird!"

Ty knelt down at her side. "Are you okay?"

Looking up, she could see the concern in his eyes. "Yeah, just a little dizzy, that's all." She started to stand.

With a hand on her shoulder, Ty held her down, saying, "No, just stay there. I was a little dizzy too for a while. Give it some time, and you'll be okay. It'll pass."

Amy and Ty. They looked up to where it seemed the words were coming from.

"This is weird!" Amy whispered. Ty nodded in agreement.

We wish to thank you for trying to keep our presence a secret . . .

Amy interrupted, "Excuse me. What do you mean 'try'?"

Ty jabbed Amy in the arm and pointed to the pond, whispering, "Look!"

Amy and Ty saw two men. One was definitely Dr. Larkin. The other looked like a campus security guard. They were wandering around the pond, looking behind bushes.

"Oh, no!" moaned Amy, her hand flew up to her mouth. "Rocky," she whispered, "will they find you? Or the tree?"

Do not worry. They cannot see or hear anything within my ancient friend. I think not. Not with the little information they have. It is far too limited. But you must not return with the notebook. You must leave it behind.

Amy did not even have to think before responding. "You've got it, Rocky! But how are we going to get out of here with them out there . . ." She took a deep breath and continued, "And if they found the park, they'll probably find us. What's going to happen to us? What will they do to us?"

That we cannot say, but we will do our best to protect you . . .

Again, Amy interrupted, "But how, Rocky?"

All that we can do would surprise you, Amy. Please do not worry. That wonderful feeling of calm she experienced after she cracked her head on the rock once again filled her.

"Amy!" She turned to Ty. He had that ridiculous grin of his working overtime.

"I love this!" He rolled his eyes and said with a laugh, "Quit worrying!"

That made Amy laugh. "Okay, okay!" She stood there, looking around. "Okay, so I won't worry . . . Rocky! But I've got a gazillion questions for you—"

Ty stopped her. "Don't ask. When it's the right time, he'll tell."

Amy frowned. "Typical," said Ty. She smiled and stuck her tongue out at him.

Feigning a moan, she asked, "Rocky, why can't I ask?"

There was silence. Amy was about to ask again when Rocky broke the silence. *For now, the more you know, the more danger you may be in when you return.*

"So . . . can I guess?" She'd spent many hours thinking and guessing. Part of it she put into her notes—things they had not told Dr. Larkin about, but he had more than likely read, and parts of it she puzzled about in her head. It had been fun. Now, she wished she'd kept it *all* in her head.

Ty tried unsuccessfully to stop her from continuing by glaring at her. Ignoring him, and without waiting for an answer, she began.

"Well, let's see. Ty thinks you're some space creature, but the more I think about it, the more I think you're native to this planet." She paused, hoping for confirmation of her theory. None came, so she shrugged her shoulders and started to continue.

She saw Ty's jaw drop. She smiled. "You never thought of that, did you, Ty?"

He shook his head. "Just what do you mean when you say 'native to the planet'?"

She continued, "Well, like *we're* native to this planet. A species that has evolved through the centuries."

"Oh," said Ty. "I thought you were going to get weird or something."

"The tree is a living species that we can identify. But Rocky, well . . . Rocky is not supposed to be 'alive,' at least by our scientific standards, so I guess our science is far from perfect." She paused momentarily before adding, "Plus the fact that we can move into this living tree, well, that one I haven't figured out yet."

"Now, the big question is," Ty quickly interrupted, "do they want our scientists to discover them?"

Ty stared directly into Amy's eyes.

"No!" His hat fell into his face as he punctuated his answer with a sharp nod of his head. "That's what I think. What about you, Amy?"

Amy started to answer Ty's question, but Rocky interrupted her, startling both of them. *It is time. Amy and Ty, you must leave—now.*

Amy jumped. "Oh, Rocky! Please don't do that!" As she looked around, she added, "Why do we need to leave now? I'm just getting used to this place. I—"

You must go now, Rocky again interrupted her. *And leave the notebook behind, please.*

She felt the urgency in his voice.

It is safe for only a little while. We will talk again soon. I promise. Now, go home to your parents—take an indirect route, please—and tell them what has happened.

Before Amy could protest, she felt something gently push her toward the edge of the tree. She dropped the notebook, and before she knew it, both she and Ty found themselves outside of the tree.

From inside their heads, they could hear Rocky speaking, *Go. Your parents will understand.*

They did not hesitate. Immediately, they ran around the pond toward the safety of the bushes. Not a word was spoken as they dashed toward home, following Rocky's instructions. Only once did Ty dare to look backward to see if they were being followed.

Thankfully, there was no one.

CHAPTER FIVE

The Telling

AS THEY APPROACHED Ty's home, they could see both sets of parents on the porch deep in conversation. The adults turned as they heard them approach. Ty could see the concern on his parents' faces and wondered what was up.

It isn't that late, he mused. An unpleasant thought poked at his mind. He turned to Amy and whispered, "What if Dr. Larkin found out where we live!"

Amy quickly whispered back with a smile, "Don't worry. Rocky said things would be okay." With confidence, she stepped up the walkway to the front porch and greeted her parents and Ty's parents, "Hi, everybody."

Trying to look as normal as possible, she smiled and, though a little out of breath, asked, "What's everybody doin'? Are we having a party tonight?" Amy thought her parents looked concerned. Ty just quietly followed her up the steps.

Mrs. Taylor stepped forward to greet her daughter. "Hi, dear. We've just been talking about Dr. Larkin." She watched Amy's face for a reaction. When she could not see any, she continued, "How did your interview go with him? Did you get the information you were looking for?"

Amy remained calm and gave her mom a hug, saying, "Well, we didn't do very well, and I left my notebook there, so we had to go back for it. Then he wasn't very nice at all." She could see her mom was looking at her, waiting for more. "Mom, is everything okay?"

Mrs. Taylor looked around at the other parents. "Amy," she paused and then added, "Ty, why don't you both sit down."

Everyone settled into chairs as she continued, "Dr. Larkin came here looking for both of you. He was pretty insistent about seeing you and stayed for quite some time. He just left about five minutes ago and asked us to let him know when you came home. Are you two okay? Please tell us what happened. Everything, please."

Amy looked at Ty who was sheepishly slouching in one of the chairs in the corner. Ty gave her a half smile and gestured in her direction, giving her permission to tell what she wanted. She gave a big sigh, turned to the adults, and began explaining what had happened. She told them all about Ty's dream, finding Rocky, and the tree. Amy figured none of them would believe her, but she continued to pour it all out. She was amazed that they all seemed so calm and serious. There were no smirks or hidden laughs. As she came to the end, she was wondering why they were taking all this fantasy with such calm.

When she finished, she sat quietly, waiting for them to respond to this outlandish story. It seemed like the silence lasted forever. Mr. Taylor looked over to Ty's father. The two of them nodded to each other, as if agreeing on something.

Finally, she said, "Well? Do you believe us?"

Straight-faced, her dad was watching her, saying nothing. The suspense was killing her. She repeated her question, "Well, do you?"

He pulled his chair up close, facing her squarely and said, "Yes, Amy. We do believe you."

Amy's body relaxed. She was glad they did believe her, but a niggling question formed as she started to wonder why.

Smiles crept onto the once serious faces that surrounded Amy and Ty. "Bet you're wondering why we'd believe such a crazy story, right?" Her dad wore the biggest grin as he chuckled, nudging her.

"How'd you know I was thinking that, Dad?" Amy looked around at the faces that were so happy and, she thought, *they look so relieved—even excited. I wonder why.*

"Well, young lady, it's only natural. But the reason we believe you is that we have all had to keep a very similar secret for so long. You see, your mom and I, along with the Graeagles, grew up in this town and chummed around together, just like you and Ty. We discovered the same thing you did when we were just about your age." He paused to think for a moment.

"No, the difference is that we only met the Guardian—that's what we called him. It was such an exhilarating experience. Only, we never told a soul, until now. Dr. Larkin is certainly not the right kind of person to let in on this secret, kids."

All the adults nodded in agreement. Ty had come out of his slouch and was sitting on the edge of his chair as each of them told their story of how they had met their rocky friend.

" . . . And for the longest time, he allowed us to visit him, but as we got older, went on to college, found jobs, and then married, we—well, we just didn't take the time to keep in touch. It must be at least twenty-five or thirty years since any of us contacted him." Mr. Taylor said that with some sadness in his voice.

"We did try to talk to him before you two were born, but he never responded. We just thought he had died or moved on to another place. We didn't realize there was a connection between him and the tree."

With a smile, Amy's mom added, "I am so glad he's still here. We did talk the town into preserving the park, making sure the trees and pond would never be developed in any way. That way, if he was still alive and hiding, he would be safe. That is one thing we were able to do as adults."

Mrs. Graeagle nodded in agreement. She had been very quiet this whole time. "It is a very special place." Her voice floated across the porch, lifting spirits as she spoke. "We made sure you both had many opportunities to play in the area. We are all so glad that it was you that the Guardian chose to open up to." She sat with her hands in her lap, smiling, eyes dancing as she nodded her head.

"Yes, it is an honor that he has chosen the two of you. I am so glad."

In amazement, Amy and Ty sat listening to their parents as they talked about their experiences.

Finally, Ty spoke up. "Mother, Father. I'm so glad that we don't have to keep it a secret from you anymore. It's been so hard." He stopped and pulled his hat from his head, holding it securely in both of his hands. "But now what do we do? Dr.

Larkin sure doesn't seem like he is going to give up anytime soon. I'm so afraid he'll find out where Rocky is."

His father put a hand on Ty's head and mussed up his hair.

In a soft voice, he said, "Don't worry, son. Rocky will be safe. Dr. Larkin will never find him, and he knows nothing about the tree. The town will not allow him to dredge the pond—even if he figures out which one it is. That is something we made sure of. You see, we were afraid something like this might come up, so when we protected the park, we didn't stop at this one spot. We made sure that all the parks in the whole town were protected equally so there wouldn't be just one that stood out as special over the other parks. It took some convincing, but City Hall thought it was a great idea, with all the 'progress' that had been happening throughout the country. They wanted to keep the small-town image, and this was a great way to do it."

He smiled at the thought that they outsmarted people like Dr. Larkin. "And there are at least four or five parks and twice as many ponds within walking distance to our homes. He's going to be extremely busy trying to figure out which one. Hopefully, he'll give up soon."

Amy's dad smiled and, looking over to Ty, commented, "Hmm. Just an observation, but I've noticed that when we were kids, your dad always seemed to connect better with our friend than any of us too." With a twinkle in his eye, he laughed. "Must be something to do with your Indian heritage, Matt!"

Ty's father laughed and nodded as he said, "Well, that may be, but I think it more has to do with the fact that Ty and I just enjoy nature more than any of you." Winking at Ty, he added, "What do you think, son?"

"I'm not sure, Father." He smiled, and without missing a beat, he said, "I think that Amy's just too busy talking. Rocky can't get a word in edgewise!"

He carefully watched for Amy's response. A smile crept across his face. He was sure what she'd say.

Amy looked flustered as she stuttered, "Well, I . . ."

Ty started to laugh as he stumbled through an apology. "Sorry, Amy. I just couldn't resist. But I think my father may be right. I spend so much time in the park and camping with him. You like to bury your nose in your books—especially mystery books."

"It's getting chilly. Let's all go inside for a bit." Mrs. Graeagle opened the screen door and gestured for everyone to move indoors. The parents went in, chatting among themselves, laughing.

Ty plopped his hat back onto his curly mass of hair, pulling it forward as he lowered his head, covering his now troubled eyes. He sighed. Moving slowly to the front step, he slid down onto it, resting his head in his hands. His hat slipped even further forward, practically covering his whole face. He didn't care. His thoughts were troubled, not feeling as safe as Amy's and his parents wanted him to feel. Just how safe was Rocky and the tree?

Amy glanced over to see Ty slip down onto the step. With their parents inside, they hadn't noticed his sudden change of mood. She settled in next to him and sat quietly for a while.

When she couldn't stand it any longer, she popped her face close to his and, with a huge grin, giggled. "What's your problem?"

As she backed away, Ty slowly raised his head, pushing his hat back, revealing the concern still covering his face. "Amy, do you really think that Rocky is safe? I mean, there aren't *that* many parks in this town. And what's to keep the professor from talking the town council into letting him search? What—"

"Ty, you worry too much!" She didn't have a chance to say any more because her parents came back out and announced it was time to go home.

"Bye—see you tomorrow, Ty. Talk to you later, okay?" She kept her eyes on his face and waited for his comeback, but none came. His concern was still there as he pursed his lips together, eyes focused on his shoes. She sighed and followed her parents back to their house.

As Amy and her parents arrived home and entered the front door, she echoed Ty's concerns to her parents. "Mom, Dad? What if Rocky and the tree aren't really safe from the professor? What if he is able to find them and talk the town council into—"

Amy's mother cut her off gently, saying, "Amy, dear. Please don't worry about it. If the Guardian thought there was a problem, he would have let you or possibly even one of us know. And if we hear of anything that might look like trouble, well, we're better able to deal with it than either you or Ty.

"Now, let's stop talking about this and get ready for dinner. I'm sure everyone is starving!"

Her mother hurried into the kitchen as she rattled off the things Amy needed to do before they could eat. Amy trailed close behind her, nodding and mentally noting all that her mother wanted. Amy wanted to call Ty to make sure he realized that everything would be just fine. She would have to put it off until after dinner. She sighed as the kitchen door swung shut behind her.

CHAPTER SIX

A Plan

THEY HAD BEEN afraid to visit the pond for the remainder of the weekend yet felt Rocky would be the only one that could tell them how to handle the possibility of the professor showing up at school. Early on Monday morning, long before school was to start, they went to the pond. They had been careful to make sure no one followed them by heading toward one of the other parks first and then back tracking to their pond, constantly watching over their shoulders for anything suspicious.

"We can't wait forever, Ty!"

They were sitting on the log when Amy jumped up. She was getting impatient, constantly looking at her watch. She was afraid they'd be late for school, and Rocky had not contacted them yet.

She turned to confront him, ready to demand they start heading to school, when she noticed that faraway look again. She could feel the excitement welling up.

She trembled and whispered, "What do you hear?" Amy put her hand on Ty's shoulder and gently nudged him, trying to get a response.

"Ty," she whispered.

With a dazed look in his eyes, he turned to her, finger to his lips. "Shh."

Then he closed his eyes, leaving Amy to wonder what was going on. After a few minutes, he finally opened his eyes, and a smile crept onto his once serious face.

He sighed, jumped up, and grabbed her arm, shouting, "Let's go!"

Before Amy had a chance to respond, she found herself running close behind Ty heading for school. All he would say is that he knew how to handle whatever came up. He wouldn't say any more. For once, she would have to put things entirely into Ty's hands. She scowled at this thought. They had always done things together. She was going to have to wait for him to tell her what happened, and the more she thought about this, the more jealous she became. Rocky was excluding her. She tried to shake these thoughts but couldn't.

They continued to run toward school, not even worrying about who saw them, and this concerned Amy. As they approached the school grounds, it was still early, and very few students were present. Ty came to an abrupt stop, and Amy tumbled into him from behind, sending him flying into bushes at the edge of the school grounds. She stood there, panting, hands on knees, trying to catch her breath.

Laughing, Ty climbed out of the bushes and brushed himself off. "Well, then. I guess next time I need to warn you." He laughed.

Then he stated in a hush, "Amy, I'm sorry. I know you're not happy with me, but I've been trying to get my head around all that Rocky said and how to explain it." He walked over to one of the benches that lined the walkway up to the school, sat down and, patting the bench, said, "Come here, and I'll try to explain. We don't have much time."

Amy reluctantly came over, still feeling hurt and left out, then plunked herself onto the bench with arms folded in front of her.

As she waited for an explanation, she thought, *This better be good.*

Ty immediately started explaining what happened, unaware of the ill feelings she held toward him right now. They talked for some time, and Amy finally started to feel better about it all when a group of their friends came up from behind, surprising them.

"Hey, you guys! After school, we're getting together at my place for pizza. My mom said we could go the park after. Wanna join us?"

Amy started to say something, but Ty beat her to it, coming back to their invitation with "Boy, that'd be great, but Amy and I are trying to get this blasted report done. You *do* remember that we only have a couple of weeks before Miss Tansy wants it turned in, right? We're supposed to go see that *professor* again."

Amy tried very hard to not look startled by what Ty just said. He was looking right at her, and she realized her mouth was wide open. She quickly shut it, hoping their friends had not noticed. They merely shrugged their shoulders, laughing off the idea of working on their own reports, and waved good-bye. They all headed off into school, leaving Ty and Amy to continue talking.

"We're *what*?" Her tone made it obvious she was not pleased. "No way am I going back to see *him*!" She was still dumbfounded by what he just said.

Ty laughed, throwing his head back a bit. "Oh, that was just to make my excuse sound good!" He didn't like lying and noticed that it seemed to come a little too easy. He didn't like that one bit.

Amy was relieved but not sure she liked the idea of lying to their friends. She certainly didn't want to have to confront that man again anytime soon—at least, not voluntarily. But lying was not the solution—it usually caused problems down the line.

"C'mon! We need to get to study hall." She grabbed his sleeve, and the two headed to their first class.

As they turned the corner to enter the study hall, there stood the professor, towering over their teacher in another fancy suit, quietly talking with her.

There was no turning back since Miss Tansy had seen them and cheerfully called out their names. "Amy! Ty! I'm so glad you are here. Professor Larkin has come by and was telling me about your visit with him on Friday! I think it is great that he was helpful—and I'm honored that he found time to visit. Did you have anything else you wanted to tell him or ask him before class starts?"

Now it was Amy's turn to shrink up against the wall, while Ty stepped forward to talk, glancing quickly at Amy as he did. Miss Tansy noticed this uncharacteristic action and cocked her head to one side. As Ty and the professor exchanged polite words, Miss Tansy started to wonder what was going on. Amy was usually the one to initiate the conversations, not Ty—especially where adults were involved. Yet she noticed how Amy backed away from the professor, and this concerned her.

She decided to take things into her own hands and interrupted the conversation. "Professor, I am sorry to interrupt, but it is nearly time for class to begin, and these two need to get into their seats. Perhaps this can be continued after school."

Just then, the bell rang, as if to punctuate the necessity for the conversation to end. Miss Tansy could hear a sigh of relief from Amy as she graciously said good-bye to the professor and scooted the two into the safety of the class, leaving the professor standing there as she closed the door behind her. In a hushed voice, she told them she wanted to talk to them immediately after science class. They nodded their heads without saying a word and headed straight for their seats, relieved that Miss Tansy had saved them from the professor, at least for now.

He stood outside the classroom, trying to decide his next move, listening to the teacher give instructions to the class. His shadow was visible through the frosted window, and Amy was very relieved to see it finally vanish from view as the morning announcements blared through the speaker.

Amy glanced at Ty, who seemed quite satisfied with himself. She gave him a scowl, and he muffled a laugh, whispering, "It's okay! It'll be fine. We just need to talk to Miss Tansy afterward and tell her everything."

Amy stared at him in disbelief. It was supposed to be a secret, and *he* wanted to tell the teacher. She was about to say something when the teacher asked for the class's attention. She quickly turned around to face Miss Tansy, sighing.

The question will have to wait till later, she thought and settled in to listen.

Each class dragged on for what seemed like forever. Throughout the day, Amy and Ty tried to figure out how to avoid Professor Larkin and found it difficult to concentrate on their studies. Finally, in their last class, they waited for the inevitable bell to ring. They knew the professor would, no doubt, be lurking in the hallway or in the yard, waiting to corner them.

As the final bell rang, everyone sat quietly in their seats, waiting for their teacher to dismiss them. Amy saw the door to the classroom opened slowly, and she held her breath, fearing the professor would slither into the room. Instead, her mom's head popped through the crack, and she quickly motioned for her daughter to come. Amy looked at Miss Tansy, silently seeking permission to leave; and when she nodded, telling both Amy and Ty to go with Mrs. Taylor, the two grabbed their backpacks and bolted for the door, without questioning it. Then she excused the rest of the students.

Mrs. Taylor very quietly herded the children to the car and drove them home. No questions were asked by her usually chatty mom, which surprised Amy. As a matter of fact, there was no conversation at all in the car. This truly puzzled Amy. She gave a questioning glance over at Ty, and he simply shrugged, mouthing an "I don't know" in return.

Mrs. Taylor dropped Ty off right in front of his house.

Amy thought this was crazy since they lived next door to each other but said nothing. She simply waved good-bye and quietly said, "I'll talk to you later, okay?"

Ty nodded in agreement as he closed the car door, swung his backpack over his shoulder, and flew up the walk to his house. From the porch, he turned to wave good-bye, but the car was already in Amy's driveway and moving out of sight to the back by their garage.

He shook his head, adjusted his cap, and opened the door to his house. He walked in and called out, "I'm home, Mother. Mrs. Taylor gave me a ride. I'll be up in my room working on homework if you need me."

He could hear his mother in the kitchen, singing beautifully along to the music on the radio as he headed up to his room, wondering if she had heard what he had said over the radio.

He mumbled, "Oh well. No big deal."

At Amy's house, her mom was getting quizzed about the unannounced pickup at school, even before they got out of the car. "I don't have a doctor's appointment, do I? You never pick me up. Why today? Is everything okay? "She gasped, "Oh! Did someth—"

Her mother calmly broke in, "No, dear. Everything is just fine. But I received a call from Miss Tansy at lunch, and she thought it would be a good idea if I picked the two of you up. She told me Professor Larkin was at school today and that she had noticed that you seemed a bit, well, shall we say, distant? She felt that was not like you. I didn't say anything to her about your run-in with the professor but agreed that I would pick you both up and deliver you safely home. She seemed relieved. Let's just leave it at that. Your dad and I will talk with the Graeagles tonight and discuss what our next step will be."

As they headed into the house, her mom continued by asking questions about the meeting with the professor, and Amy filled _r in as best she could, but her mind began to wander. She no longer heard anything her mom was asking.

She was wondering about the professor. *Was he going to keep coming to the school until he could talk to them? What were they going to do to 'take care of it'? Would that be enough?*

Amy's wandering mind was interrupted by her mother. "Amy? Amy!" Her mom laughed. "Honestly, young lady. Please pay attention."

Once her daughter was finally able to focus on what she was saying, she sighed and added, "Oh, honestly, Amy. We'll talk about this later. You obviously have your mind elsewhere. Why don't you go work on your homework for a while? Then you may come and help me by setting the table for dinner." Her mom was shaking her head.

Amy nodded her head and mumbled an apology, "I'm sorry, Mom. I was just thinking about the professor . . ."

"Yes, I know, dear. Let's just get the homework out of the way, then set the table. Oh—and then it would be great if you'd help me get the last bit of dinner put together. Would you like to make a salad? Or perhaps you'd like to choose the dessert tonight?"

Amy jumped at the opportunity to choose the dessert. Then she grabbed her books and flew up the stairs to work on school assignments, contemplating what dessert she would make.

CHAPTER SEVEN

The Rendezvous

AMY WOKE WITH a start from a deep sleep, sitting straight up in bed. She went to bed easily enough after an enjoyable dinner and routine evening with homework and the like—her family even found time to play a few games of Scrabble. She'd actually forgotten about the trouble from earlier in the day. But now, as she wiped the sleep from her eyes, it dawned on her. So much had happened that it hadn't really sunk in about what they saw while hiding inside that tree.

That countryside. Inside a tree? Amy mulled that peculiar thought over in her mind. *It has to be an alternate universe or a portal to some other part of the earth—or something!* She really didn't know what she saw, but it excited her.

She scowled as she glanced at the bedside clock—two o'clock in the morning! She moaned.

It's the middle of the night, and I can do absolutely nothing about it until morning! As she looked up and stared at her ceiling in the dark, she fell back onto her pillow and sighed.

Slowly, an idea formed at the edge of her mind. A smile grew larger and larger as the idea grew and became firmly planted. She popped back up, looking around her room in the dark, trying to remember. Throwing her sheets off, she jumped out of bed and dropped to the cold floor on hands and knees, poking her head underneath.

Groping around with her hands at the backmost part, she triumphantly announced in a whisper, "Ah-ha!"

She dragged a shoe box-sized container out from under her bed and sat there for a moment, trying to think things through.

Amy carefully took off the dusty lid and felt around until she found the object she sought. Pulling the metal flashlight up to her, shivering at the coldness of it, she crept over to the window and opened the curtain. She could only hope that Ty was having as sleepless a night as she!

Very quickly, she threw open the window, cringed at the loud noise it made, and froze in place. She listened in the quiet of the night for any evidence that she had been heard. When she was assured that it was safe, she pointed her flashlight at Ty's window and flashed it on and off three times. She paused for a minute and then did it again. She did this three times before she saw a silhouette drag itself to the frame of the window, slowly sliding it up so not to make a sound.

Ty looked funny in the dim light cast by her flashlight. His hair was askew on top of his head. She laughed quietly because it reminded her of the famous photo of Einstein—like he put his finger in an electrical socket.

"What the heck!?" he croaked in a loud whisper. "What's up, Amy?" As he rubbed his eyes, he demanded hoarsely, "For cryin' out loud! Can't this wait till morning?"

She didn't answer. She just pointed down to indicate he should meet her at their emergency spot and then disappeared.

Ty shook his head. He wondered what she was up to . . . He only just barely noticed the lights flashing on his bedroom wall. He had not been able to sleep. Tossing and turning, he'd been thinking about the recent days' events and his parents' apparent feeling that everything was under control. Yet he had an uneasy feeling that wouldn't allow him to sleep and wondered if this was what kept Amy awake as he slid the window shut quietly.

He threw on his robe and slippers and worked his way in the dark down the stairs, avoiding the creaky boards so not to wake his parents. Slipping out the kitchen door, he crept into the side yard, then the backyard to the fence line. He pushed one of the boards to the side and carefully inched his way between them until he was into the open field behind his house where Amy's shadowy figure hovered nearby.

Concerned but a bit irritated, Ty whispered, "Amy, what on earth is the matter with you? This is for *emergencies*. Are you—"

Amy cut him off, "Yes, yes . . . I'm okay."

There was a pause, and he almost started in again with his questions but thought better of it.

"Ty, I've been thinking . . ."

He was glad it was difficult to see his face. He'd been frowning the whole time. His voice certainly expressed his disapproval at this late-night rendezvous. Now he regretted it. Amy's voice had a mix of fear and excitement.

"Our parents seem to think that they can handle Professor Larkin," she whispered, "but what if they can't? And"—she took a deep breath before continuing—"and I'm wondering about that tree we went into. Do you realize that we know absolutely nothing about what we saw? Rocky never *did* tell us anything about it. Yet"—she swept her hand before her, though completely invisible to Ty because of the lighting—"there was this alternate world or some sort of portal to another place, and we didn't even *think* to investigate! Didn't even cross our minds! What's with that? Why do you think I'm just remembering it now, Ty?"

Ty had been patient as Amy threw question after question at him. He now took the opportunity to interject his thoughts.

Yawning, he said, "Ya know, I couldn't sleep much because I was thinkin' about this too! I'm worried about Professor Larkin. I don't think he'll quit—*especially* now that he knows where we live and where he can find us at school. But I do think we have Miss Tansy on our side, so we're safe at school."

Ty thought a minute. He could only see Amy's silhouette. Her head was down. "Amy, are you okay? I don't really know what to say about that other world thing we saw. For some reason, everything is fuzzy, but I do remember a little bit now. I don't know why I didn't remember. It *is* coming back, bit by bit. More like a dream. I—I don't understand why. And . . . you're right. Why didn't we try to explore?"

Ty paused for a moment to gather his thoughts. "Well, maybe because we were so worried about Professor Larkin and your notebook. *And* Rocky was, to say the least, insistent on our getting home."

Amy looked up at him and laughed. "Yeah! You're right! We *were* slightly preoccupied with trying to escape from the professor after he got hold of my notebook." She shook her head.

"That was *so* dumb—putting *all* our discoveries in that notebook and then bringing it with us to the interview. *Really* dumb! Oh, well. We can't undo that dumb move, can we?"

Ty yawned again. "Look, Amy. We both need to get back to bed and rest. I think tomorrow is going to be a busy one. Besides, we don't want our parents to find us here. Let's leave for school just a little early and go see Rocky. Let's see if he wants us to do anything, okay?"

Amy whispered, "Yes."

She was not quite sure that would be a good idea, but she said nothing more, and the two parted, sneaking back into their respective homes, back into their warm beds.

As she nestled back under her covers, she thought she heard someone calling to her. She quieted herself, listening intently.

"Nope. My imagination, I guess," she sighed.

Then she heard it again. This time, she smiled. She recognized the voice. It was Rocky. She almost squealed for joy. Rocky actually contacted *her*! Not Ty, but *her*. She smiled to herself but was startled by the urgency of what she heard next.

Amy! You and Ty must not come to see me tomorrow. I will be in touch with you. We are not safe if you come to the park. You are not safe either. The professor is watching you.

The voice faded as it repeated, *The two of you are not safe. We are not safe. Not with the professor. Talk to your teacher.*

Amy was shocked to hear the last bit.

Not daring to speak, she scrunched up her face in concentration, thinking, *Talk to Miss Tansy? But, Rocky! Break our promise to our parents—and you—and telling Miss Tansy? Rocky, explain! Please explain!*

There was nothing more to hear. Only the silence of the night, and her shallow breath answered her as she strained to hear anything in reply. She was worried about what Rocky just told her, turning it over again and again in her head until she finally drifted off to sleep.

The next thing she heard was her mom telling her she'd overslept. Amy tore the covers off and quickly readied herself for school.

Ty was waiting for Amy as she rushed out of her front door with her mom following closely behind.

His quizzical look brought shrugging shoulders from Amy as her mom announced with a cheerful greeting, "Good morning, Ty! It's such a lovely morning. I thought I'd walk with the two of you as far as the school. I have an errand to run at the general store."

Amy, with her back to her mom, rolled her eyes and made a grimace. Ty laughed and winked at Amy as he turned to her mom. "Glad to have you join us, Mrs. Taylor!" Lowering his voice, he added, "We were going to stop by the park, though."

"No. I don't think that would be a very good idea," interrupted Mrs. Taylor as she nodded toward the unfamiliar car parked just a half block away.

"Let's just get you two to school, and if Miss Tansy is there early, let's go have a chat."

"Um . . . Mom, I . . . I think that's a really good idea." She spied Ty's reaction.

Ty's mouth dropped wide open in protest. He looked over at Amy. He could see she was just as surprised by her mom's comments but was doubly surprised by Amy's response. His mouth remained wide open.

Smiling, his friend reached out and tapped his chin. Ty immediately closed his mouth but kept his eyes riveted on Amy.

She continued, "So do you think that we are *not* safe as long as the professor is poking around? And if he's following us, then Rocky's not safe if we go visit, right? But, Mom, why go see Miss Tansy?"

As Mrs. Taylor rushed the two along, she whispered, "This is not the time nor place to discuss any of that. Let's just hurry and get you to the school so we'll have time."

Amy opened her mouth to ask more questions, but before she could, she heard something in her head. *Amy, do as your mother says—hurry. No more questions right now.*

She glanced at Ty and realized he must have heard it too from the reaction on his face. She nodded as the three of them hurried down the sidewalk toward the school.

As they entered the classroom, there stood Miss Tansy, as if she was waiting for them. There was a distinct look of concern on her face as she approached them, quietly greeting all three and closing the door. She mumbled something to Amy's mom and told Amy and Ty to have a seat in the back of the room, away from the door. They cast questioning glances at each other but obeyed. The two adults exchanged a short whispered conversation before they both came over and sat next to Amy and Ty.

Miss Tansy cleared her throat quietly and glanced at Mrs. Taylor before she started. "We are in agreement. You *are* in danger . . ."

She raised her hand to stop Amy from interrupting. "Please, let me finish. What your parents did not explain the other night is that there are more of us than just your parents that know about the creature you are calling Rocky. Quite a few—we're not sure how many or even who everyone is since each was sworn to secrecy. Each of us, in our own way, has worked quietly to protect him from being discovered."

"I didn't realize, until it was too late, that you might have discovered him. He is very particular about to whom he makes his presence known. There must be something very special about you two. He told me last night about the dangers, and all your parents and I have been working on a solution."

She stopped momentarily, as if listening for unwelcome visitors.

Amy took this as an invitation to speak. "Rocky told me to tell you everything, Miss Tansy." With head hung low, she said it with a deep sadness in her voice. She was starting to realize just how much danger she and Ty had put Rocky and the others in.

Glancing over to Ty, she continued, "We didn't know he'd be found out. We thought we could do all this without anyone finding out."

Ty was absently nodding his head in agreement. He said nothing. Amy glanced back at him. She knew that look. She wondered to herself, *With all that's happened, do I say anything?*

Her thoughts were interrupted as her mom put a hand on her shoulder. She turned to look at her mom who was watching Ty very closely.

Uh, oh . . . she thought. She started to speak, but Ty broke the silence first. Everyone was watching him as his eyes cleared, and he started explaining what had just happened. He had their full attention as he explained what Rocky wanted them to do. Amy was amazed adults were actually listening to what Ty was telling him—as fantastic as it sounded—and it seemed as though they were willing to do what he said, even though she thought she detected some raised eyebrows at one point. It didn't bother her anymore that Rocky had not given these instructions to her.

She smiled at the realization of this change in her. The jealousy was almost gone. She was glad those feelings were no longer dragging her down. They were all working together to protect these very special creatures.

Whatever it took, she thought.

"Okay," said the teacher with determination, "let's do this! Elizabeth, go back home and let the others know the plan. They can each get their part of the plan begun while we"—she looked at Ty and Amy with a smile—"get on with our part!"

The two students beamed at the thought of spoiling Professor Larkin's investigation.

Amy's mom waved a quick good-bye and left as the first students drifted into the classroom, completely unaware of the extraordinary thing that was about to happen. Amy and Ty took their seats, and Miss Tansy made her way to the front of the class, busying herself with routine duties until the bell rang.

The car Mrs. Taylor spotted earlier was now parked across the street from the school when she nervously stepped off the school grounds onto the sidewalk. She turned toward her house, wondering if it would follow her or stay and wait for the children. She was almost relieved to hear the engine start up, and although she dared not look back, she was now sure she was the chosen target.

After a short while, she fumbled for something in her purse and deliberately dropped it so she could glance back down the street. She was alarmed when she could not find the car on the street. Then she had second thoughts. *Perhaps this is better—now the children are safe, and I can do what needs to be done without them poking their noses in it.*

Satisfied with that thought, she swept up the item she'd dropped, stuffed it into her purse, and hurried home to call her husband, Ty's parents, and one other person she'd been unaware that shared their secret.

This is sure to start a chain of events! She smiled at that thought as she entered her front yard, nearly running up the steps to her house.

After making one final glance before slipping inside, she locked the door for the very first time in her life. She frowned as she pulled her hand away from the lock.

"I can't believe I just did that!" she said aloud, then busied herself with the list of things discussed at their quick meeting.

"What did you say?" Her husband popped his head around the corner to see her gasp and put her hand up to her face, turning a deathly shade of gray.

"Ooh! Don't do that, Michael!" Regaining her composure, and as the color slowly returned to her face, she added, "You nearly scared me to death! What are you doing home?"

Mr. Taylor apologized, "I'm sorry, Liz, but I could have sworn I heard the lock turn." He glanced at the door, amazed, then continued excitedly, "He's talked to me, Liz. He actually talked to me! He told me to be home as quick as possible, so here I am. What's going on? Why is the door locked? Are they here?"

She shook her head as she headed for the living room phone. "No, but we need to prepare. Let me explain . . ."

CHAPTER EIGHT

The Surprise

AT LUNCH BREAK, Amy and Ty asked to stay inside to work on their science project, and Miss Tansy was busy preparing for a special activity.

Amy whispered in a hoarse laugh as she laid down her pen, "Ya know, we *do* have to get this report done . . . for real. But I sure can't focus. What about you?"

Ty was too busy. With his head still buried in the papers in front of him, scribbling notes, all he said was "Almost done. Just a minute more." With a final flourish of his pen, he exclaimed, "Done!"

Miss Tansy looked up and, without asking, put her hand out. Ty scooped up Amy's just as she put the finishing touches on it, and with his paper, he tidied them both, handing them to the teacher.

She quickly glanced at them and said, "Excellent! Good job, both of you. Now, go outside, but please stay close to the building—just in case. I'll see you in class."

They nodded and obeyed. They wasted no time and went to hang out with their friends.

"Where the heck have the two of you been—teacher kept ya from comin' out?" One of their friends playfully pushed at Ty, and he just laughed it off.

"No, we finally finished our report. We were so close to being done that we asked if we could finish it during our lunch break." He laughed, then added, "And she thought it was pretty cool, so she's got something special planned for our class!"

Amy chimed in, "Yeah! It *sounds* like a field trip! Cool, eh?" She glanced around at their friends. She knew they'd love to get out of schoolwork with a field trip, no matter what it involved.

"Neat!"

"Cool!"

"Way t' go, guys!" plus a couple of pats on the back were the responses they received as the bell rang, ending their lunch period. Each headed to their next class, looking forward to seventh period.

Everyone worked their way into the science classroom, with Amy and Ty coming in last, after everyone was already settling in. The second bell rang before they slipped into their seats. Their usually vigilant teacher ignored their tardiness and made her announcement.

"All right, everyone. I've been busy getting approval from the principal and contacting your parents for permission to go on a short, impromptu field trip this afternoon." Several whoops and hollers were heard before everyone quieted down again with

Miss Tansy standing, waiting patiently for silence. "Now," she continued as she scanned her students with a hint of a smile on her face, "a few of your parents will be here shortly to help out. We are going to walk to a park for a bit of a biology lesson."

She spun around to grab something from her desk, and a few groans could be heard as she turned back with a handful of papers. She quickly distributed them to the first student in each row. "Now, you may take one and pass the rest back. There's not much time. You will take these with you to the park and search for the items on the list. This is part of Amy's and Ty's report. They were kind enough to finish their report early so we could have this field trip."

Ty and Amy could hear their fellow classmates shift in their seats to better see these two traitors—the two classmates that pushed more school work onto them so late in the year! Ty could feel their stares and felt himself sink noticeably lower into his chair. Amy, on the other hand, remained straight and tall in her seat, smiling.

Several of the students' parents slipped into the classroom as Miss Tansy continued to talk about what was expected of them and exactly where they were going. Amy's mom and Ty's father were among the parents that came to help. All the parents gathered into one corner and listened carefully as the teacher spoke. Finally, Miss Tansy turned to the parents, thanked them for coming on such short notice, and asked the students to line up quietly. As they did so, she asked Amy and Ty to come forward to lead the group.

They came forward, each with several sheets of paper in hand. When the door opened and they filed out, the parents, one by one, took up their positions peppered among the students, with Miss Tansy in the lead and Ty's father at the end. He firmly closed the door behind him and followed the line from the school grounds toward one of the parks.

He could hear the engine of a car start from behind him and slowly pull out from its parking place. It did not turn to go the opposite direction. Nor did it pass them. Mr. Graeagle frowned.

CHAPTER NINE

The Announcement

A S THE ASSEMBLY of students, parents, and teacher arrived at the park entrance, a van with a large antenna and the local TV station logo plastered on the side came up alongside of them, waved, and drove ahead to the park's parking lot. Two men poured out of the van, pulling camera equipment and microphones from the rear.

Mr. Graeagle smiled and chuckled to himself, *She sure knows how to do this right!*

Miss Tansy waved and walked toward the crew as everyone busily chatted among themselves, wondering.

After a few minutes, she came back to the group of students and adults, with the two men following close behind. The taller man, well dressed in a smart gray suit and tasteful blue tie, held a mic in his left hand. It was obvious he knew how to carry himself without looking too flashy. A shorter, heavyset man in rumpled jeans and a dingy green T-shirt followed behind him, lugging a large camera on his shoulder.

Miss Tansy made a sweeping motion toward the taller man, introducing him. "This is Mr. John Kelvin. You may recognize him as one of the reporters from our local television station." Everyone bid him a polite hello as Miss Tansy introduced the other man. "And this is his camera man." She hesitated.

Mr. Kelvin jumped in with "This is Mikey, my camera and sound man. Couldn't do it without him!" He flashed a big grin that extended to his steel grey eyes and nodded. "I understand you are going in search of some treasure."

There were gasps and whispers among the students.

Miss Tansy laughed and shook her head. "Oh, well, I guess you could say that! We have a list of things they are going to try to locate in the park for the science unit I am teaching. I am so glad you thought it would be wonderful to show them at work on their field trip."

She turned to her students. "Mr. Kelvin and I both love science. Though I grew up here, we went to college together and became good friends." A couple of giggles and snickers could be heard, but Miss Tansy ignored them and continued, "And we both *happened* to end up in the same town after we graduated."

Mikey adjusted the camera on his shoulder and cleared his throat, directing his question to Mr. Kelvin. "Can I take a shot or two, John?"

Mr. Kelvin glanced around and noticed a car parked down the street and could just make out the shape of a man in the driver's seat, hunched over toward the passenger seat, looking busy doing something.

"Sure, Mikey. Get some good shots of the kids, and why don't you pan around down the street a little too?"

He smiled as he looked over at Miss Tansy and Mr. Graeagle who quietly came up beside her, whispering in her ear. She nodded her head to Mr. Graeagle and smiled back at her friend. The parents, by this time, had started to move the students into the park, with Mikey following close behind them, taking video of them as they went. As he panned back down the street toward the parked car, the figure ducked down below the dashboard. He continued to film for a few seconds more, then panned back toward the classmates, scattered by now, searching for their list of items. Mikey followed and recorded them as they called out their discoveries and dutifully scribbled their answers on the sheet of paper given to them by their teacher.

Miss Tansy and the parents carefully guided them toward a pond with an old, large tree overhanging it. The tip of a rock just peeked its head above the waterline, fortunately, out of harm's way. There was a grassy spot nearby the edge, and it is this place that the adults wrangled the students, and Miss Tansy asked them to take a seat.

She asked if everyone had found all the items on their list and was met with a resounding yes. Mikey kept recording the moment for the reporter, panning back and forth, to make sure he had all of them included. He panned a little off to the left of the group because from the corner of his eye, he could have sworn he'd seen the bushes move. He kept the camera going, scanning the bushes with its lens, but when he saw nothing more, he slowly panned back to the group, repositioning himself to get a better shot of the teacher. She laughed at the students' responses and continued, asking what kind of things they found. Without waiting for her to call on them, shouts of "oak trees," "trillium," and "water lilies" were among the responses she received.

"Excellent!" She now motioned for Ty and Amy to step forward.

After Miss Tansy quieted her students, Amy and Ty stepped to the front, looking around at everyone, then at each other. An occasional croak could be heard here and there in the pond behind them. Amy nodded, and when Ty sighed quietly, she nudged him.

He cleared his throat and began nervously, "First of all, Amy and I want to thank Professor Larkin. Without his help, we would never have known all the stuff we had to do when we found our animal for the science project.

"You see, we found a very freaky looking frog. He's orange in color and has five toes on *all* four feet. We've researched frogs, like Miss Tansy told us and found out that for this area, the color wasn't normal and usually indicated a poisonous frog. And usually, there are four toes on the front feet and five on the back feet. So we decided he's either what scientists call a mutation, or he is a new species." There was a buzz from their peers as they heard this news. With a smile on his face, Ty continued despite the noise, "So we looked around and actually found four of them here in the pond! Amy and I figured that it probably wasn't a mutation."

At this point, as Amy stepped forward, she noticed a shadowy figure in the bushes out of the corner of her eye.

Without missing a beat, she proudly continued where Ty left off, "So after going to the college and talking with Professor Larkin, we came to the conclusion that these frogs must be a new species—at least, new to this area. We are going to need the professor to make sure we are right, but we're almost certain it's true."

As the two stood there proudly, their friend Mike had a question and wasn't waiting to be called on. "Hey! Does that mean you'll get to name the frog? Isn't it the tradition for the guys that discover something to name it?"

Hands shot up and waved frantically in the air, only a little more patient than Mike, actually waiting to be called on. Ty pointed to one. "So where are these frogs? Are we going to get to see them?" Everyone chimed in, agreeing.

Miss Tansy stepped forward. "Very good question, Mike— and Glen." She paused, looking around at the excited group. "And everyone else, just be patient. Everyone *will* get a chance to see this frog. But we must be careful. Since we don't know just what it is—new or mutation—we need to take care around the pond to protect its environment."

Turning to Amy and Ty she continued, "So *we* will stay here and *patiently* wait while they go find one in the pond." Satisfied for the moment, they began to talk among themselves while they waited. The two discoverers tippy toed toward the pond and whispered to each other as they went.

Ty whispered, "Don't look now, but Rocky is getting ready to send us the frog. I sure hope this works." Amy and Ty saw the rock in the pond quiver ever so slightly.

Pointing to a weedy spot at the pond's edge away from the rock and heading for it slowly, Amy whispered, "I hope this distracts them, but don't worry. Rocky and Miss Tansy know what they are doing." Tiny, almost invisible ringlets ebbed out and away from the rock.

As if on cue, a single frog began to sing in a high-pitched croak from the weedy patch where Amy had pointed. Everyone stopped talking, and the two could feel eyes fixed on their progress. Ty pulled the rubber gloves from his pocket and put them on, tucking his long-sleeved shirt into the edges of the gloves.

He could hear Miss Tansy explain, "Ty is doing that because many times, brightly colored animals indicate that they are poisonous in some form. They may excrete some poison or have a poisonous bite to defend themselves from predators . . ."

Ty focused on what he was doing and ignored the lecture going on behind him. Amy slipped her gloves on, and the two slowly approached their unsuspecting victim. It gleefully sang its high-pitched croaking song and then was joined by two or three others.

The two hovered over the patch for a moment, speaking quietly to each other, "On the count of three . . . ," and nodded.

"One . . . two . . . *three!*" Both dove down upon their colorful little frog, capturing it with four hands.

Ty shouted, "Got it!"

Everyone cheered, jockeying for the best view. Miss Tansy and the parents quieted and corralled them, requesting they line up if they wanted to see the frog, reminding them to resist the temptations of touching the frog. Miss Tansy pulled a clear plastic box with breathing holes in it to house the frog from a bag she was carrying. Ty deposited the frog into the box, and his classmates began the slow process of examining the creature.

Although John Kelvin was busy taking notes, while Mikey was taping the entire proceedings, the newscaster saw a shadowy figure in the bushes and was trying to keep an eye out for it without looking too obvious. It stayed in the bushes, just barely visible, watching all the action. Once Ty announced the capture of the frog, the figure slowly disappeared into the bushes.

Miss Tansy glanced in the direction of her friend, motioning for them to come closer. Mikey stopped taping, and as the two came in close, Mikey repositioning himself to capture some good close-up shots of the frog and the students observing it.

Mr. Graeagle could see, from the corner of his eye, a lone figure with its head down, moving from the parking lot and making its way toward the group. He whispered to Miss Tansy again and quietly backed away from the group, discreetly working his way in the direction of this figure. Smiling, he could see that the man was dusting himself of leafy debris. He knew full well that this was the professor and that he was the individual they had seen skulking in the bushes earlier.

"Professor Larkin?" The well-dressed professor jumped at the sound of his name, startled to find one of the parents standing in front of him.

"Um, yes," he sputtered. "I am Professor Larkin. And who might you be?" He collected himself up, ready for this confrontation.

"Aah, sir, my name is Matthew Graeagle. My son is Ty. He and a classmate came to see you about something they'd discovered, seeking your guidance. You dismissed their findings."

He paused to allow this information to sink in a bit before continuing, "Then"—he raised an eyebrow as he watched the deadpan face of the professor—"all of a sudden, you show up at Amy's house and make inquires at school asking about everything. And now, you are here. Seems you are interested after all, eh?"

The professor shifted uneasily on his feet and glanced beyond this man to the group of children and adults before responding to Mr. Graeagle. "Hmm. Seems you have me there, sir. I realized that they may be onto something, so I needed to inquire at the school to find out more."

"Yes, indeed. And now that they've found it, my son and his classmate are more than willing to turn their findings over to you, sir. Come." With that, he raised an arm, as if to invite him to continue on toward the gathering. With Mr. Graeagle following behind, Professor Larkin straightened his jacket, did a last minute dusting of his sleeves, and headed toward Miss Tansy.

The teacher watched, and as they approached, she turned and greeted him warmly. "Professor Larkin! I am so glad you could make it. I left a message with your assistant, but it sounded as if you were unavailable."

She turned to the circle of students, all crowing around Amy and Ty, jockeying for a chance to get a close up look at the captive amphibian. "Class, please make room for Professor Larkin. He graciously helped Ty and Amy, so he needs to take a look at the frog."

The professor sputtered in protest, but when he saw Mikey swing the already recording camera to face him, he mustered a pleasant smile and straightened his jacket again as he made his way through the cluster of children.

"My!" was all he could say when he saw the caged amphibian. He went straight for it, mesmerized by the oddity before him.

"Definitely something special, this is," he mumbled with a smile, holding the Plexiglas container at all angles to get a good look at the little frog.

So entranced by this discovery, he did not hear the newscaster walk up to him, talking into the mic and camera, introducing the professor.

"Professor Larkin, would you say that this is a new finding for the scientific community?" Mr. Kelvin shoved the mic into his face, expecting a response. When he realized that the professor had not heard him, he cleared his throat, nudged him, and repeated the question.

"Professor, can you tell us if this is a new species?"

The nudge jarred him from his mesmerized state, bringing him back to the task at hand. Collecting his thoughts for a quick response and so he could be rid of the reporter to go back to examining the delightful creature before him, he smiled.

"Sir, this is a very rare find indeed, but to be certain that it is truly a new species, well, that will require a closer examination at my lab." His attention quickly turned to Ty and Amy who had patiently stood by during the professor's examination.

"Just where did you find this creature, and is this the only one?"

Before either Amy or Ty could answer, he bombarded each with many more questions, leaving little time between to answer. Miss Tansy came to their rescue, stepping in and carefully answering each question, satisfying the professor but not giving away their secret.

At last, the three of them gave the professor permission to take the frog away, cage and all, back to his office at the college. As an afterthought, he thanked them and dashed off, clutching his prize, toward the parking lot and his car, appearing quite content.

Mr. Graeagle came up alongside his son, tousling his curly hair as he reached for his shoulder. He tapped Miss Tansy on her shoulder with his free hand, smiling.

"I think it worked, yes?" His grin broadened, and his eyes danced with delight at the thought that they had rid themselves of the professor so easily. "They are safe. At last!"

Miss Tansy said nothing but nodded in agreement.

Ty looked at his father, then his teacher, trying to read the unspoken conversation he thought he could see between them.

Amy chimed in with a whisper, "Yes! Finally, we can be sure the professor will now concentrate on this pond, not Rocky's. I am so happy!"

She waited for them to agree.

Though slow to respond, Miss Tansy said, "Um, yes, Amy. I do believe they are safe—" Without saying anything further, she turned immediately to gather her students for a fast return trip to the school. Time passed too fast, and it was nearly time for school to let out. The parents and teacher gathered everyone, including Amy and Ty, to head back to school before the last bell rang, leaving John Kelvin and Mikey to quickly wrap up their piece for the news channel before they gathered their equipment into the truck. As they drove off, passing the group, they waved and said good-bye.

Mulling over his teacher's last comment, Ty knew there were unspoken words. *For the time being*, he thought.

He could hear a rumble of confirmation from their friend in the back of his mind. "For now, we are safe."

Edwards Brothers Malloy
Thorofare, NJ USA
November 25, 2013